# QUENCHED

## A ROMANTIC VAMPIRE FANTASY SERIES

PARCHED
BOOK THREE

## Z. L. ARKADIE

FLAMING
HEARTS

ISBN: 978-1-942857-36-5

## CHAPTER I

# THE HOUSE OF BENEL

T t's pre-evening. My fingers and the tips of my nose and ears are freezing. I could remedy this with a shield of warmth, but right now I want to *feel* the earth.

I'm walking up 1$^{st}$ Avenue. In only a matter of days, the snow will layer the trees planted along the sidewalks. Usually I relish in this time of year because I like to watch the white ice rain down. But I'll miss this season of snowfall and many more after—maybe hundreds or even thousands of them. I'm on my way to Enu, and it doesn't snow there.

Never in my life have I nursed this sort of broken heart, but certainly, that has changed. As each step takes me closer to the Enu portal, the blood-pumping organ in my chest aches more and more. I can't imagine remaining on Earth while knowing Baron Ze Feldis is in love with another Selell. I can't go back to my day job, either—not as long as Lang, Bender & Jenison Advertising, where I worked four years ago as executive creative director of fashion and beauty, maintains an account with Red Yard, Baron's energy drink company.

Last night when I looked Baron in the eyes for the final time, he was entering a Red Yard event at the Met here in Manhattan. I imagine my old firm gave him his money's worth and put his company on the map. So much has happened between us in the last three—almost four—years, I never stopped to wonder what sort of everyday life Baron lives.

These are the things the public knows about him: he's rich, super-sexy, and dating a woman who looks like a supermodel. These are the things I know about him: he used to love me, but for some strange reason, he doesn't anymore, which makes him a very good deceiver. *He once said he would love me forever*. That brings me to the fact that I know he's a vampire and the world doesn't. Yes—he's the perfect deceiver. *Now my heart aches even more.*

The city streets are bustling like usual. It's dusk, so those who put in extra time at the office are hoofing it on the sidewalks, wearing heavy coats and layers of clothing. Their warm breath generates misty clouds of frost in front of their faces. They can't see me because I created a veil of invisibility over myself, but I can see and hear them; I know what they're thinking and feeling.

A time existed when I too was worried about what was for dinner, tomorrow's meeting, and the many other practicalities of life. But never again. I'm going to be gone for a long time. A day in Enu is nearly a year on Earth, so who knows what this world will look like when I return a hundred years from now. I'm committed to discovering just that.

I hear, *Is that all it takes?*

I look around, trying to locate whoever said that.

*The lives of millions sacrificed because you're grieving over Ze Feldis?*

"Who are you?" I ask out loud.

A tall, thin woman wearing a dark-green scarf whips her face toward the space I left behind.

*I'm on your shoulder.*

I look and see the black-and-white polka-dot butterfly creature.

*You're the Wek*, I say but not out loud this time.

*I am a Wek*, it asserts.

3

I take another glance at the creature. The first time I saw and heard it speak, I'd thought I had lost my marbles. That was also the first time the blinding fog rolled into Manhattan, the day Baron Ford—who I now know as Baron Ze Feldis— returned to my life five years after we first met.

*You didn't answer the question,* the Wek reminds me.

*I don't know what you mean by sacrificing the lives of millions,* I reply quite curtly.

Two fire trucks scream past us, blasting their sirens and casting flashing lights against the tall buildings. Cars try to navigate to the side of the road to let them pass, but traffic is too thick. Now horns are honking all over the place. It's chaotic.

*The prophecy of the Seven Seeds is unfolding; this is not the season for you to return to Enu,* the Wek says.

My pulse accelerates, but my pace slows. I see myself back in Ethiopia at the burial sight of my five-thousand-year-old actual paternal grand- mother, Zillael. I feel myself being stabbed through the back by Zina all over again. She was a deranged vampire who would rather have killed me than let Baron love another woman. I'm also seeing how his two silver-bladed daggers sealed her fate. Wounded, I dragged myself to my grandmother's grave and recovered the Script that tells of our future. I'm the only daughter who's able to translate the writings. I have the Power of Mind, and I'm only beginning to scratch the surface of knowing the scope of what that power is.

I sigh with a renewed sense of resolve. I know there's more of the Script for me to read, more battles to fight. Although I'd rather run home to lick my wounds, I've been burdened with the task of guiding all seven sisters to our final destiny.

I stop in my tracks to glare up at the lofty, glass-mirrored United Nations building. I remember standing here, on days long past, doing just this—admiring how nearby skyscrapers reflect on its mirrored skin. A lot has changed since then—a lot.

*I remember the Script and know it's unfolding,* I finally admit to the Wek on my shoulder.

*Then what do you choose, Cl'auta, fifth daughter of the House of Benel?*

I twist my neck to study the Wek. What a strange thing it is. Its beady white eyes are watching me.

*Where next?* I whisper.

We're riding the wind, whizzing past the tops of tall skyscrapers. This still feels unreal, as if I'm living in the pages of a comic book, like Superman over Metropolis or Batman swinging through Gotham City.

We journey northeast, over dense woods and small towns. The sun continues to dip westward. We're slashing through a familiar forest. Soon we'll reach the house where my sister Fawn lived with a man who was once a vampire. Lario Exgesis became human again, then transformed back into a vampire. My sister loved him, and he betrayed her.

We come to a grinding halt at the edge of the property. I gaze up at the sky. There's my glowing protection shield left over from the last time I was here, but a second layer blankets my initial broken coating. The new sheet is resilient, blazing blue, and casts a light over the entire property.

"Did Felix do this?" I ask the Wek.

*Yes, he did.* The butterfly-like creature flutters its wings, lifts off my shoulder, and charges forward. *Follow me.*

We bolt out of the tree line and cross the field of plush green grass, which is a lot healthier than before. The house is Tudor-style with gray brick walls and a roof covered with black shingles. I can feel the emptiness of the inside—it's just swallowing me up.

The front door opens on its own the moment I step on the gray cement porch. My senses are heightened; the last time I was here, I had to save my sister from her demented boyfriend. I found Fawn curled up on the floor of an underground prison built with walls of silver to keep her *in* while keeping vampires *out*. Lario was brokering a deal with another Selell—her blood in exchange for transforming him back into a vampire. To keep the vampire interested in the pact, Lario supervised little taste sessions of Fawn's blood. Visualizing how *that* went down only infuriates me more.

But this memory is interrupted by the lights cutting on. I see that Lario's entire collection of books is gone. Actually, the entire place is empty. The furniture is gone. The grandfather clocks are gone.

"What happened?"

*The books have been secured*, the Wek replies.

"And the clocks?"

*They've been secured as well. Everything else has been searched and either kept or destroyed.*

I stare across the room at the empty bookcase that opens to an elevator shaft that descends to the depths of the property. My pulse races. When I was here before, in the belly of this house, I energized Fawn with enough power to help her fight back. Instead of using that power to blast off Lario's head, Fawn used it to shove him into the prison he'd kept her captive in. That was after he begged her not to kill him in a pathetic display of cowardice. Before I could reach into his heart and snatch the leaf from the Tree of Life, the vampire he'd made a deal with had begun the process of changing him back into a Selell.

But I was the one who'd had a moment of weakness. The sheer horror on Fawn's face, the way wanting to kill him and save him tortured her, made me suggest she put him in her prison. During that rare flash of anger that afflicted her, I should've urged her to finish him off.

"Is he still here?" I ask. "Lario Exgesis, I mean." I stare daggers at the bookcase.

"No, he isn't," the Wek answers. "But I must show you something."

I look quickly to the left and see a man standing beside me. Then I glance at my shoulder. The butterfly is no longer there.

"I'm Lorenzo, the Wek," he answers before I can ask who he is.

I can't look away from Lorenzo. His skin is a vibrant russet, and his eyes are sable but bright like the moon. Everything about his face is soft: nose, cheekbones, jaw, and chin. He's feminine but masculine, a stunning creature.

"This is my humanoid form," he explains.

I study his inflections. He sounds the same. Deliberate with his words, but lacking a harsh tone. He'd make a great PR person. His voice could convince people that all is safe and secure, even while their house is obviously on fire.

"Wow," I marvel, stunned by this reveal. Finally I'm able to refocus. "You said you were going to show me why you brought me here."

Lorenzo nods and steps toward the bookcase that hides the elevator. I can't stop watching him. First of all, he appeared in his human form fully clothed, and I wonder how that could be. Were his hair fibers actually clothes? But there he is, wearing a white T-shirt that gently kisses the ripples of his chest and a pair of white cotton pants. He moves gracefully and powerfully, like a prize-winning stallion.

When the bookcase slides across the wall and the elevator opens, I'm still studying him. I'm trying to find a flaw—nobody's that perfect. At least, that's what I'd thought until this being graced my eyes.

"Cl'auta," he says, nudging me on.

I blink myself out of this state of fascination and trot across the floor to enter the elevator. The pit of doom feels just as bleak as it did before, maybe worse since I'm here in my full physical form. Like the upstairs, this room has been gutted. The cot Lario laid upon while being changed back into a vampire is gone, and the silver chains no longer dangle from the doorway of the silver-walled prison.

"And what happened to Lario?" I ask.

"The prison didn't contain Exgesis because he wasn't a full Selell."

"Which means he crawled out of there," I conclude past gritted teeth.

"That *is* the case."

"So he's free?"

"He's free."

"Then where is he?" I ask. I want to hunt him down and bring him to justice.

"He's lost on Earth."

"Does that mean he can't be found?"

"Yes."

"Did you try?" My tone is unintentionally harsh.

"No," he answers calmly.

"Did Felix try?"

"He's not permitted to search for Exgesis in the earth realm. Only the Seven Seeds can enact his power upon the beings of Earth."

I have six sisters; I make seven. Each of us has a power. I have the power of the mind. Fawn has the power of force. Adore has the power of light. I've yet to meet my other four sisters. Some of us live on the earth; some live in Enu. According to the prophecy of the Seven Seeds, one day we will all meet, and that's when the full power of the House of Benel will be unleashed.

I give the room another once-over. I'm frowning so hard my face hurts. "I don't understand why he went through all of this. From where I stand, it looks like he flipped a coin, and we came up on the wrong side of it."

"On the contrary. Exgesis knows the scroll has been found."

"But it's in Enu."

"The scroll couldn't stay in Enu because it's made of earthly materials. Exgesis knows it's being read, and if it's being read, then you are working to fulfill the prophecy."

My heart stops. That's news to me. I just left Enu two Earth days ago. The scroll is a remarkable piece of textile. It's made of a papyrus-type material, and the symbols and words are burnt onto its surface with a black dye.

Lario hadn't been with us when we fought and retrieved the scroll. He couldn't tag along because we rode the wind along the eastern coast of Egypt, through Sudan, and into Ethiopia. Being human, he couldn't walk on air with us; however, he did insist that we return the *book* to him. What he hadn't known was that Felix had already warned me to return our findings to him and only him. I kept my father's directive from Lario and Fawn, since he could hear everything she was told. Of course, Fawn hadn't been privy to that detail until I told her. Another deception on his part.

"Then where is the scroll?" I ask.

"I'll show you," Lorenzo says.

He walks right through the wall that's opposite the elevator. I hesitate. For a second, I wonder if my eyes just deceived me. Of course they haven't. Anything and everything is possible these days. So I follow him into a dusky portal lit by flaming sconces attached to the thick crystal walls. The fresh scent of untainted oxygen lingers in the air. I look at the surface I'm moving across at a rapid pace; it too is made of crystal. We're not in Enu, but the essence of that world surrounds us on this peaceful journey. No threats linger before or behind us. This sanctuary feels like a warm hug.

After a few twists and turns, we reach a dense, white vapor mixed with light. I walk through it, following Lorenzo, into an open-air vestibule and climb a cloudy stairway that shoots straight up. Tree branches lord over us. We step out into the woods. The climate is warm and clammy, nothing like the cold November day I just left.

"The tunnels touch on the edge of Enu," Lorenzo says. "Any mortal who enters will die."

"What a security measure," I mutter.

I can't take my eyes off the bulbous trees, rich and green. Birds are singing. There's a blue one and a yellow one, and I do recognize the red robin. They're all perched on the branches, observing us.

"Are we somewhere in South America?" I ask, remembering that birds migrate south in the winter.

"This plane is positioned on the northern tip of the state of Vermont."

I flinch, taken aback. "Well, did we pass through

the winter? It was freezing cold and close to night-time in this part of the country fifteen minutes ago."

"The time-variance continuum under the veil of the protection for the House of Benel is slightly behind the Earth's rotation."

"So it's summer here?"

"The end of July."

I look at the sky; storm clouds hover. Now I know why. However, that's it for an explanation. Lorenzo starts off, and I follow him. We pass poplar, cedar, oak, and pine trees. There are other types too, maybe maple and birch. After about a mile, we stop in front of an iron-rod fence that easily stands a hundred feet high. Sprawling evergreens are planted behind the bars; the needles of neighboring trees weave into each other, forming a curtain. I can't see a thing behind the green thistles, not even one centimeter of space.

I search left and then right for a gate or some other formal entryway, but I don't see one. "Are we able to go behind this?"

Without replying, Lorenzo scales the bars as easily as a spider climbs the bark of a tree. He doesn't have to order me to follow; I know the drill. I take a deep breath and remind myself that this is real and I have the ability to copy his movement.

I jump and grab the bars. Reach by reach, I pull myself up. Once I flip over the top, exerting great body control, I drop to my feet. There's barely any impact on my knees. Every time I push myself to these supernatural limits, I have to remind myself not to be shocked. Only the smallest part of me is human. The bigger part of me is Enuian.

My wide eyes fall over an expansive château-styled, cream-colored mansion with a steeple-topped roof that gives the place an enchanting appearance. There are also lots of high-arched windows, and bay doors cut from fine glass are positioned behind protruding iron-rod terraces. We're standing on a full lawn of pure green grass, adorned with fountains formed out of pillars of water gushing from spouts dug in the soil.

"This is the House of Benel, built for the seven daughters of Felix Benel," Lorenzo says.

He continues forward and I follow. The inside is just as lavish as the outside. I study the design in the stained-glass domed ceiling that covers the foyer, but Lorenzo gives me no time to figure out what's taking place in the scene or admire the way the sun sets the colored glass ablaze.

As we journey through the hallways, we pass lots of rooms. One section seems to be designed in the modern American Minimalist style. The limited amounts of angular furniture in bright colors sit on high-glossed hardwood floors. There are abstract paintings on the walls, shag rugs, and lots of wiry floor lamps. I wonder to whom that area belongs.

Then there's an abrupt shift, and it's as if we're back in seventeenth-century Europe: heavy curtains, golden chandeliers, Mediterranean-designed rugs, bulky furnishings in the Baroque style, a highly-glossed white marble floor. The rooms are far from my tastes, although beautifully executed.

We walk a while before getting to the end of the hallway. We step down a spiraling staircase set before a glass wall that displays the view of a majestic park. The footpaths are lined by pruned shade trees, and benches face a shallow, man-made waterfall. When we arrive at the bottom of the stairwell, we come to a closed door.

"Tell it to open," Lorenzo instructs me.

I nod, think *open*, and it opens. We enter a ball-room-sized room, sectioned by the sort of white columns found in museums or libraries. But my attention turns to an area where three long brass-colored leather sofas join in a U-shape and face a wall stacked with books.

"Wait. Are those Lario's?" I ask.

"Yes."

I nod and turn to get a view of the back of the large room. I see a pillar with the Script laid across it, encased in a chamber that's set high off the ground and surrounded by glass walls.

"There it is," I whisper. I must confess that I'm choked up. What's written on the Script was transcribed thousands of years ago by the hand of my paternal grandmother, alive before a man named Noah weathered a devastating flood. She was told by an angel that she'd have a son and seven granddaughters, who would bring her heart's desire to fruition. My grandmother wanted redemption for the evil people in her settlement, and what she received was far more reaching than she could ever conceive.

Of course, it sounds insane and too off-the-wall to be true. But it is true. I'm walking on air. I'm traveling out of my body. I can find anyone in the world if I think about him or her. I can conjure shields of protection and ones that change emotions. I can do much more, things I haven't even tapped into yet.

"So Felix brought it here," I whisper.

"Are you referring to your father?"

I shrug. I don't think I've ever called him "Father." Even when I believed I was fully human and Freda was my mother, I rarely referred to him as "my father."

"In the House of Benel, it's proper to refer to Felix as your father," he explains, definitely correcting me.

"Okay." I frown, wondering if the Wek is serious.

He's looking me in the eyes with his lips slightly parted, indicating that he's waiting for me to amend my words before he continues speaking.

"I mean, my father," I say.

"Yes, he brought it here," Lorenzo responds right away.

I was right; he was waiting for me to correct myself! I'm embarrassed and amused at the same time. My mind goes back to Viesel Egos, the divine being of few words who expected me to communicate with him via telepathy. That shouldn't have been a problem, but like Baron Ze Feldis, I'm unable to read Viesel Egos's thoughts or emotions—although I don't believe he possesses any of the latter.

"The Script is safe behind the diamond chamber. Only the daughters of the house can enter it," he continues as if nothing strange happened.

"Wait." I point at the chamber. "That's made of sheets of diamond?"

"Deep from the belly of the Rwenzori. It's the only element that can be found on both Earth and Enu. Though we can't transport diamonds from our world to this one, we can transmit the power of our world into the element of diamond."

I'm intrigued. My mind is racing.

"The evil knows the scroll has to be kept on Earth," he continues. "It will always search for it, but as long as it's kept here, in the diamond, it cannot be found."

I used to be very afraid of the evil. But after winning the battle against it at the gravesite, I'm less frightened. Ignorance breeds fear, and now I know how to fight it; it's weakened by the light.

"May I?" Lorenzo raises his gorgeous brown hands. He's asking permission to press them against my temples.

"Yes, you may," I answer just as formally.

And he does. "Watch what I've watched."

In an instant, I see a swamp. I breathe in the murkiness and smell the rot. I'm suspended over stale water, the knees of bald Cyprus trees protruding from the dingy pool beneath me. Then my eyes narrow at a sight I can hardly believe. Bodies rise to the surface, hundreds and hundreds of corpses. There are two-pronged bite marks on the necks of the dead, but these are no human carcasses. One body I study is a male. His top lip is pulled back over his teeth, and he has canine fangs. He's a Selell; they all are.

I pull back to look around me. The entire swamp is filled with them. That's when Lorenzo removes his fingers from my temples. I'm sure my horror is reflected in my eyes. I stare at him, lost for words.

"You do know that if a Selell drinks another Selell, it dies," he says.

"Yes, I heard something to that effect."

"But the vampires who did this aren't dying."

"I don't understand," I admit, although I think I would understand if I could get all those bodies floating in the swamp out of my mind.

"The rule has been broken, Cl'auta, over and over and over again."

Finally my mind works. "Which means the rule has changed?"

"No." He looks me in the eyes.

I know he's waiting for me to think it through, so I continue. "If the rule hasn't changed... Then that means there are now exceptions to the rule."

"Yes," he says as if I'm on the right track.

"And you're showing me this because somehow I'm connected to it."

"Yes."

"How?"

"What did I show you before we arrived?"

"Okay..." I nod, thinking. "Lario escaped. He's a vampire who once ate a leaf from the Tree of Life."

"Exactly," he says, pleased by my response. "When Exgesis was transformed into a Selell for the second time, he could no longer be an average vampire."

"I can't prove it, but I bet he knew that," I growl. I hate him.

"He may have or may not have. Consult the Script, Cl'auta. It's your greatest weapon against the forces of evil."

Finally, I get what our whole tour was about. It was designed to get me back on track, take me back where I left off so I may continue forward. I stare into Lorenzo's glassy eyes. This time, once I start, there will be no stopping until *we* reach the end. Baron Ze Feldis won't be around to distract me.

## CHAPTER 2

# ḦALF OF ṀY ḶIGHT

T enter the diamond chamber to consult the Script while Lorenzo sits on the sofa. It seems he's staring at the unlit fireplace. What a strange person he is.

I start by searching it for a way to stop Lario right away, but by the length of the writing, it appears I've—we've—got a long way to go before that happens. Nothing in the middle or bottom of the scroll makes sense to me. Strangely, the Script seems to only reveal its meaning to me incrementally. So I start from where I left off.

There's the leaf. There's Fawn. I save her. She lives, and Felix is able to return the gift of light, granted to all the daughters of Benel, to her. After

Lario stole Fawn's humanity, Felix was forced to take away her light. During those years, she wasn't able to enter Enu, nor could Felix contact her. Lario Exgesis had shared part of her existence—essentially, they were one, and she was not whole.

I see that the leaf, which was taken out of Lario, must be put into a gaping hole, like the one in the Forest of Naught in Enu. From what I read, that's where the leaf is now. The only part that gives me pause is that I should have planted it there, and I don't remember doing that.

That's all I see at this point regarding the leaf, so I read on. There's an image of a human heart. It's dripping blood. Then in symbols that form words, it reads: *The blood swallows the blood*.

"Okay," I whisper, putting this detail on the list of things I already know. Lorenzo just showed me that vampires are drinking vampires, and the heart that's dripping blood is written in the same context as the leaf. The blood-dripping heart is tied to Lario.

Another being is tied to Lario. It's represented by a word that translates to red encircled by six stars. Four of the stars are four-pointed; two are five-pointed. As I read on, I get that this red with the stars surrounding it is supplying Lario with his power. I think it's some sort of magic because he's using this power to search for a fang that pierces the sun.

I want to shout, "What the heck does that mean?" Instead, I stay composed and press onward. I've already determined that the fang is a vampire. I search the entire Script to see at what rate this symbol appears. It comes up quite a bit, as well as the bloody heart. Lorenzo and I were right: two types of Selells are out there these days.

I look out the translucent diamond wall at Lorenzo, who's staring back at me, but I'm not really focusing on him. I'm merely thinking. I have the ability to find Lario and stick with him, follow him wherever he goes. Why isn't that written in the Script? *Maybe it is.* So I read on.

The fang…

The heart…

The blood…

Lario…

That's all I get. I feel as though I'm missing something that I need to move forward.

When I walk out of the diamond chamber and into the main room, Lorenzo stands, watching me.

"For the most part, it's showing me what I already know. The only new piece of information I have is that Lario's searching for a vampire who has the power of the sun, whatever that is," I say with a sigh of defeat. "I guess if I can find Lario, he'll lead me to this vampire."

Lorenzo watches me with a blank look. He has a great poker face. My theory is that I can't hear his thoughts because he has none.

"Then that's what you should do," he says very calmly.

I hesitate as I sit on the sofa. I close my eyes and conjure up even the tiniest detail of Lario's face. Nothing dramatic happens when I arrive at my destination—I just appear near the intended target. It has never been difficult.

But this time, I fight against a strong red force field. All I can see is murky red fog. I push against it, and it pushes back. I use the light within me to gain ground, and we get caught in an explosive battle. The light allows me to make progress, but I'm still losing the fight. I see Lario's white hair, black eyebrows, and pale skin, but it's all fuzzy. I can't keep this up, so I open my eyes and accept defeat. I'm pretty sure that was not Lario's energy I battled.

"Something's fighting me," I say, panting. My

head feels as if it's gone a couple of rounds in a boxing ring.

"Did you use the light?"

"Yes, but it didn't get me very far."

"Do you think you used *all* of the light at your disposal?"

"I used everything I had."

"Did you?"

I think until I get what he's insinuating. We sit in silence as I fight what I know is the logical next step.

"So you see," Lorenzo says. "You can't dismiss Ze Feldis."

I bury my face in my hands. "I can't face him right now."

"Now is the only time you have."

I shake my head. "This is so cruel." I'm already chastising myself for being weak.

"Cl'auta, not only does Ze Feldis wield the light, but he's known Exgesis since the day he became a Selell. You still trust Ze Feldis, don't you?"

I lift my face and swallow. The wound he inflicted hasn't even begun to scab over. Seeing Baron now will probably kill me. Now I'm reprimanding myself for being melodramatic. *You can do this, Clarity. Mainly because you have no choice.*

BARON IS NEVER HARD TO FIND. I ONLY HOPE THE day will come when the memory of him fades so completely that I won't be able to recall the contours of his maddeningly sexy face.

There's no sunlight in the room he's in, just shadows playing off the glossy surface of the desk in front of him—a desk that must have cost thousands. I stand silently behind him, watching the three men seated across from him. Michael Colton, my ex-boss; Peter Root, the vice president of Major Accounts; and Sanford Giles, executive creative director of Consumable Products.

Sanford is noticeably fidgety. The room is chilly, but a sheen of sweat glistens across his forehead as he tugs at his collar, clearly unnerved by Baron. His unease is palpable, so much so that he can't shake the irrational fear that this meeting might end like a scene from a slasher film. He's even seriously questioning whether Baron could be a vampire, though he keeps reminding himself that vampires aren't real. Funny how instincts work.

"She took off on vacation and didn't come back," Peter Root says, picking up the thread of the conversation they were having before I arrived. His tone is biting, dripping with condemnation. There's no mistaking who "she" is.

All three men are picturing the same person.

They're talking about me.

"No, no, she's still working for Felix Parker, with um…" Michael Colton snaps his fingers as if trying to recall the details. "The Cork Group." He aims a finger at Baron, who must've asked about me.

"That's right, handling acquisitions," Peter confirms, nodding along.

I half-expect Sanford to chime in with some snarky remark, but instead, he stays silent, tugging harder at his collar, clearly too unsettled to speak.

"Sounds like she's doing well, then," Baron says, glancing over his shoulder. He doesn't see me, but I know he senses my presence.

Michael lets out a facetious snort. "She's beautiful, so…"

Baron must have frowned because Peter immediately tries to smooth things over. "She's quite striking," he amends quickly, trying to make Michael's flippant comment sound more appropriate. After all, you don't want to offend a client with a multimillion-dollar account. "And clever."

"That's true," Baron agrees, his voice cool but steady. "She is clever and beautiful."

Michael, ever the nosy type, presses further. "How are you two acquainted? You never explained."

"College," Baron replies sharply, not looking up from the papers in front of him, his tone clearly signaling an end to the topic.

But Michael, not one to leave well enough alone, asks, "Did you two date?"

Baron looks up from the papers, his focus shifting to Michael. I had just seen the intensity of his glare through Sanford's memory—it was indeed terrifying.

Panicking, Sanford shoots out of his seat, stammering, "Is there a restroom nearby?" He twists awkwardly, searching for the exit, clearly forgetting where it is.

"Yes," Baron says curtly, pointing toward the door.

Sanford strides out, eager for his escape, and I seize the moment. It's time to reveal myself. I step around the desk, my pulse quickening. Baron's profile comes into view, every angle sharp and familiar. When he turns his head slightly to the right, his eyes lock onto mine. He sees me.

"Where is it?" Sanford asks, teetering on the

edge of full-blown panic. His face is flushed, his features pinched with anxiety.

*Hi,* I say in Baron's head as I quietly stop behind Michael and Peter.

"Out the door, up the stairs, and to the left," Baron answers, tearing his gaze from me to respond to Sanford.

Michael, curious, twists around in his seat to see what Baron is staring at. Realizing how strange it must look, as if he's been gazing into thin air, Baron quickly refocuses on his business associates.

"Look, I think you're doing an excellent job," he says, his tone signaling he's ready to wrap up the meeting.

*I'm sorry to barge in like this, but I need to speak to you about Lario,* I say to Baron in his head.

"Okay," he says aloud to them, glancing at me. "Let's go another two years. Just send the paperwork to my lawyers."

*Can you meet us at the condo at sundown?* I ask.

"That's what we wanted to hear," Peter says, stretching his arm across the table for a handshake.

"Yes, I'm happy to oblige," Baron replies, addressing both them and me.

I watch closely to see if he'll shake Peter's hand,

and he does. Peter doesn't flinch, which means Baron's hand isn't ice cold. Interesting. I wonder if he's thirsty. He doesn't look like he's in need of a drink, and there's no sign of exhaustion. Are he and his pretty little girl-friend seducing humans and feeding off their blood?

That's when I open my eyes.

"He'll meet us at sundown at the condo in New York," I say to Lorenzo.

---

A SUMMER THUNDERSTORM POURS DOWN OVER THE property, and I step outside to stand in it, watching how the rain mixes with the water gushing from the sculptures. I came out here to think. Before, when-ever anxiety hit me like this, I'd walk the streets of Manhattan, preferably at night.

I close my eyes, trying to conjure the lights—streetlights, traffic lights, storefront lights, the salt-and-pepper glow of the skyscrapers at night. There were so many colors, so many distractions, that they made me forget I existed for a while.

But now, I can't shake the fact that very soon, I'll see the man who rejected me just a few nights ago. I looked so pathetic, watching him saunter up the steps of the Metropolitan Museum with his supermodel vampire girlfriend. What a cliché. A stinking, horrible cliché. I hate that I need anything from him.

My heart begs my brain to find another way. Maybe there's a clue in the books. Maybe I can reach out to Fawn—she must know something about what Lario might be hiding. She has to.

But then Reason, my old and often annoyingly practical friend, reminds me that it would take days to search through all those books, and Fawn is still recovering from a devastating attack. No, Baron is the only logical choice right now. So I take a deep breath, open my eyes, and head inside, dripping wet.

I find the space tailor-made for me on the third floor. Standing at the door, I take in just how enormous it is. It feels like living in my own private home, with my "room" spanning three stories.

On the top level, where I am now, is a cozy parlor with two burnt-orange chaise lounges facing a floor-to-ceiling glass wall—or maybe it's a diamond wall. Either way, it perfectly frames the icy mountain range outside. The plush cream carpet beneath my feet feels soft and luxurious, so I slip off my shoes and wiggle my toes through it. I love carpet.

Down a short set of block stairs to the second level, I see a dark-chocolate wood sleigh bed with a fluffy mattress and crisp white linens. The walls are lime green, one of my favorite colors, and large triptych oil pieces, featuring nature scenes, decorate the walls. I step up to the bedroom porch's railing to look out over the bottom floor, which is a patio with romantic accents and comfy chairs facing a diamond-stone fireplace.

Felix sure did get it right. I love this space, and the décor distracts me from the dilemma that's now returned to the forefront of my mind. I must prepare myself to meet Baron Ze Feldis.

I strip out of my wet black slacks and shirt, and I carry my wet clothes until I find a walk-in closet/dressing room. There's a hamper near the door, so I shove my wet clothes in it and then go rifle through the racks. Every article of clothing I own is here, everything that Freda ever forced me to buy or bought for me.

I put my hands on a nice, simple black wrap dress. But as I lift it off the bar, I remember it's the same dress I wore that night in Cambridge with Baron. I put it back and opt for a slinky, navy blue wrap dress. It's cold in the real world, but a comfortable dress relaxes me. I throw on a pair of knee-high black leather boots and a long trench coat to keep me warm.

When I get downstairs to the main foyer, Lorenzo is there.

His eyes gloss over me before he says, "Our travel time through the tunnels will have to be one minute twenty-four seconds to arrive in Manhattan by dusk." He sounds and looks so serious.

I respond with a formal "All right then."

We head out across the lawn and over the dense trees. Lorenzo and I are always quiet, and what's great is it's a comfortable silence. There's no pressure to chitchat.

Once we pass through the wall comprised of blinding light before entering the tunnels, I ask him, "Why isn't there a portal in the house?"

Lorenzo just looks at me for moment and then takes off in an all-out sprint. Remembering the time constraints, I take off after him. The sconces attached to what I now know are diamond walls pass by in a blur. Our path includes a series of twists, turns, and long straightaways. We open up to a woody part of Central Park.

It's chilly, but that never keeps the natives indoors. Lorenzo transforms into the butterfly, and I initiate a protective shield over myself. The sun has already dropped, but the sky is still bright purple. The deepest parts of the park are almost empty, but once we cross the reservoir, the joggers, dog walkers, and leisure strollers are thick on the ground.

Although the tunnels allowed us to travel at a record speed, the Earth's atmosphere slows our pace. The nearness of Baron hits me when I arrive at the front door of the apartment building; that's where I make myself visible. Lorenzo lands on my shoulder as I use the key card I put in my coat pocket to open the door. I bypass the elevator and run up twenty-three flights of stairs in seconds.

As soon as I enter the hallway to my old unit, I feel him even more. Baron Ze Feldis is here, waiting for me. I pass a former neighbor of mine. I've seen him a number of times, but I never took the time to learn his name. He's balding and is probably in his mid- to late-forties. I usually saw him late at night, after I put in long hours at the office or returned from a walk. He was always tripping down the hallway with women half his age, and it didn't take much to ascertain that he was rich.

He nods at me because it's been over four years since we've seen each other. I nod back with a gentle smile. Normally he snubs me because he knows a woman like me can't be bought. He used to force himself to believe I was a stuck-up "bitch" who never "got any" and would probably die an old spinster. Even back then, none of that scared me. What's wrong with being alone? The moments I spent alone were the most peaceful.

But since I've gotten a taste of love, I do fear being without it. Love was like experiencing the high of my life and hoping to never crash. But I crashed. And the man who caused that collision is right behind my door.

I brace myself by closing my eyes and taking a deep breath. Then I hear someone speaking to me.

"You haven't been here for a while."

I open my eyes and look to my right. The guy's come back, and his intentions are loud and clear. He wants to ask me out to dinner, and he's hoping for a little dining on me after we eat.

"No," I say. I'm shocked and kicking myself for not keeping up the boundaries. My smile gave him hope.

"So did you get married while you were gone?" He's grinning, reading my expression.

His teeth are very white, but I smell cigarette smoke on his breath. I glance at the butterfly on my shoulder, wondering if the man sees it. Wearing a live butterfly would be strange for most people, but Lorenzo doesn't even distract him.

*Are you invisible to him?* I ask Lorenzo in my head.

*Yes, I am invisible to the human eye in this form.*

I find myself nodding at Lorenzo's answer.

The neighbor flinches as if he's taken aback. "Oh, you did get married?"

Before I can answer, the door to my apartment swings open. Baron stands on the threshold, glaring at the man for a few seconds. Then he puts his eyes on me.

"Hi," he says forcefully.

After seeing the glory that is Baron Ze Feldis, the neighbor is thinking of a way to make the quickest exit. The moment is definitely awkward. I turn to the neighbor, whose heart rate just shot up. He feels something ominous about the tall guy with warrior-like beauty.

"I'm sorry, I didn't get your name," I say.

"Jerry," he mutters, tearing his eyes away from Baron's face. He looks at me, but he's not seeing me. His survival instincts have kicked in.

"Jerry, it was nice seeing you again."

"Yeah," he barely says. He walks away so fast he's almost running. He glances over his shoulder once before he opens the door to his apartment, hurries in, and closes it.

I hear the bolt lock. That leaves Baron and me almost all alone, still staring at each other. Goodness, he's sexy. He smells good—like mint and lime and a hint of black licorice. He's still wearing a crisp white shirt and perfect-fitting black trousers. Truly, the man is a sight for sore eyes.

If there was ever a perfect man for me, he would be it. At this moment, I feel the doom and gloom of being alone for the rest of my life. I know there's only one Baron Ze Feldis on this Earth, and he's bonded to a vampire.

"I should go inside," I barely whisper.

But he doesn't move. He just stares at me with no distinct expression. So I step forward. That's when he moves back, careful not to touch me. He smells even better up close. When I walk past him, I feel a familiar warmth and tingling stir inside of me.

Baron has been waiting in the dark, so I flick the light switch on in the living room. Dim, orange light chases away the darkness and makes Baron look even more striking. I want to look away and remind myself that I've already cut my losses, but I don't want to show him how broken my heart is. I want him to see that I've moved on. So I stare right back at those penetrating eyes.

"How are you?" he asks.

"Good," I answer unconvincingly.

We're locked in this awkward moment. Baron's eyes don't shift away from mine until they narrow on the insect on my shoulder.

He grimaces. "Is that a butterfly on your shoulder?"

That's when Lorenzo flaps his wings. We watch him take a turn around the room before he stands beside me in human form.

"I'm Lorenzo," he says.

Baron's eyes shift between Lorenzo and me. I see all the questions in his expression; although we're no longer together, I'm still unable to read his mind. I still wish I could.

"I'm the Wek." Lorenzo puts his hand on my shoulder, and Baron's eyes expand as he stares at Lorenzo's hand. "And her watcher."

"Why does she need a watcher?"

"Because she's one of the Seven Seeds of the House of Benel; the Power of Mind."

Baron's frown deepens as if that answer did not suffice.

"Listen," I say to get us back on track.

But Baron's eyes still pick Lorenzo apart.

"Baron?"

Finally he looks at me, although both sides of his mouth are turned down.

"What do you need from me?" he snaps. "You have a watcher."

"It's simple," I snap right back. "You're friends with Lario, and I need to know where he is. Just tell me, and we're done." Saying that hurts my heart, but I don't quiver or show any signs of pain.

"Exgesis is not my friend."

"Does that mean you don't know where he is?"

"Maybe I do."

"Can you tell me where *maybe* may be?"

Again his eyes shift between Lorenzo and me. "Why?"

"Because I need to find him," I reiterate.

"Alone?"

I catch his quick glance at Lorenzo. I would think he was jealous if he hadn't told me he'd fallen in love with another vampire and ended with *Oh, and by the way, stay safe*.

I feel myself losing it. "Maybe. If you tell me where he is, then I'll determine if I can go alone or…"

"You cannot go alone, Cl'auta," Lorenzo cuts in.

Both Baron and I stare at him. I'm surprised he chimed in with that assertion, and Baron seems to hate that he spoke to me at all.

"Okay, then you're coming with me?" I ask Lorenzo.

"No!" Baron shouts with a growl in his throat. "I'll take you."

"What?" That's something I did *not* expect to hear. My mouth is agape; I'm too confused to respond verbally, but I rapidly shake my head.

Lorenzo touches my shoulder, and Baron scowls at his hand again.

"If I don't take you, then you're going to have to find another way," Baron declares, his jaw set in defiance.

I've never been a stubborn person, nor combative, nor unreasonable. My *ability*, as I've always called it, has gifted me with the talent to be the peacemaker. But at this moment, I want to dig in my heels. I want to fight Baron Ze Feldis. However, his offer is my only option. Using the power of the Encaser to find Lario failed, and now he knows I'm looking for him. I have no time to screw around.

Yet I can't help giving in to my impulses. "No."
I narrow my eyes at Baron's beautiful face.

*Cl'auta, do you remember the light?* Lorenzo asks me.

*Yes,* I say back without taking my eyes off Baron.

*Ze Feldis still holds the light, and you need him for that.*

I whip my face toward Lorenzo. "There's no
other way?"

"No," Lorenzo affirms.

"No other way for what?" Baron growls.

"Tell her, Ze Feldis," Lorenzo says. "When was
the last time you were thirsty for blood?"

I look at Baron for the answer, but he doesn't
answer right away.

"Tell her," Lorenzo insists.

"Since that day… When you came to me at the
Met."

I'm lost for words. He shunned me, so how can
we still be bonded?

"You are the daughter of Felix of Benel, Clarity.
You were born with a purpose, but so was Ze Feldis.
Just because you two have shattered your sexual
vow to each other—"

I wince. "It wasn't only sexual." I sigh to regain
my composure. I'm letting my emotions get the best
of me. "Okay, regardless of how I feel about what

you just said, you're saying that Baron and I should go hunting for Lario together?"

"Because both of you wield a portion of the power of light," Lorenzo surmises.

When I glance at Baron, he's staring at me so hard his eyes make my heart flutter. I want to touch him. More than that, I want him to touch me. I see where Lorenzo may be right, but I'll never admit it out loud—never.

"This is just so unfair," I grumble.

Lorenzo gently takes me by the chin and lifts my face. I don't have to look at Baron to know how stiff he's gone.

"Don't be sad, Cl'auta. You are making all the right decisions."

"Could you remove your hand, please?" Baron blurts.

Without hesitation, Lorenzo does as he asks and nods. I cannot believe Baron is jealous. I've experienced that in humans. When they've loved a person, it's hard to completely let go. It *is* good to know that I meant that much to him. *At least.*

"I'll leave now, but I'll see you soon," Lorenzo says. In a snap of a finger, he transforms back into the polka-dot butterfly.

Baron and I watch him fly right through the

glass window. When we're alone, we stare into each other's eyes. I don't know what he's thinking, but I'm wondering what to do next. I'm also wondering how to stop my desire to jump into his arms and taste his sweet mouth.

"So where are you taking me?" I say in a cracked voice.

Baron's eyes veer toward the hallway to the bedroom and then back to me. "You'll know when we get there."

"Really?"

"Yes, really," he replies, mimicking my hard tone.

## CHAPTER 3
# THE LONGEST SHORT TRIP

I t's hard to believe that Baron Ze Feldis actually owns a sleek white Maserati with dark tinted windows. Right now, he's driving twenty miles below the speed limit, and I'm staring out the window with my nose close to the glass. Traffic on the New Jersey Turnpike is a killer.

After we'd decided that we would head out together to find Lario, he asked me to give him an hour to return with our transportation. I said yes but had my suspicions about why he needed an hour to secure transportation. We could've ridden the wind or called a cab, but I assumed he was returning home to pack and inform his girlfriend where he was going. I thought of what he might of have told her—maybe that he's taking a business trip that came up all of a sudden. He didn't know how long he'd be gone, but "I love you, and I'll be thinking of you every second." Just thinking about it infused me with jealousy.

But when I'd said I'd take the hour to return home and throw a bag together in case we were gone for more than a day, he strongly objected and insisted he'd provide whatever I needed during our trip. If he hadn't put his hand on my shoulder, as he used to before we broke up, then I probably would've asserted myself. His touch discombobulated me, and all I could do was sit on the sofa for forty-five minutes, figuring out how to get through twenty-four to forty-eight hours alone with Baron Ze Feldis.

So when he'd knocked on the door and we walked down to the Maserati parked at the curb, I was a tad shocked. Baron doesn't strike me as the sports-car-driving sort of guy. I've never pictured him driving, actually. It's sort of strange watching a man, who I know can travel from Vancouver to Cambridge in a matter of minutes, driving a car.

"Are you comfortable?" he asks.

I don't turn to look at him. "I am."

"Do you listen to music?"

"No, I don't." I'm not being difficult; I don't listen to music. I don't know why, I just don't.

We turn silent again, but I feel his energy demanding more of my attention. I can't believe he's trying small talk. I'm determined to not say another word to him.

"Have you eaten?" he asks.

"No."

"Good, I'll call in dinner for you. What would you like to eat?"

"I don't need to eat."

"You don't?"

"I'm only a quarter human, remember?"

"I remember, but you have to feed your human side, don't you?"

"Not if it's not hungry." I'm being snippy, and I hate it. It takes too much energy to be mean to someone who's trying to be accommodating. "I'm sorry. I'm not being a nice person, and you are."

I don't understand why he looks at me with that same blank, penetrating stare that makes my heart flutter. One thing I've learned over the years is that a woman likes a man to stare into her soul—if she's attracted to him. *Oh, God help me, I'm still so very attracted to him.*

"You don't need to apologize to me, Clarity—ever."

Not knowing how to respond, I stare out the window again. I hear him skip a breath as he cranks up the speed.

"We'll be at Teterboro soon," he whispers.

"All right." I glance at him, not wanting to be rude again.

I think he discerns my intention because he glances at me with a very dubious look on his face. If he still knows me as well as he did three years ago (probably a week ago for me), then he realized how insincere I just sounded. I take a shallow breath, reminding myself again that this will be a very long *short* trip.

Baron navigates the Maserati past the checkpoints and right to the flight strip. A sleek silver jet awaits us.

"Is this yours?" I ask as we remain in the car, bracing ourselves for the next leg of the journey.

"Yes."

"So you can afford this?"

"I've been alive for a long time, Clarity. I should be able to afford this, don't you think?" He gives me that smirk.

I want to chuckle at his response, but all I can

do is stare at him while breathing heavily. I think I see him take a sniff of me.

"I *do* think," I finally reply with a weak smile. I grab the door handle.

"I'll get that for you," he says.

Before I can object, he's out of the car, and my door swings open. The cool night air is a welcome change, releasing all the tension of being close to Baron. We walk up the ramp to enter the silver jet.

The inside looks a lot like one of Felix's jets, but this one has two flight attendants. My father's fleet doesn't have any, which I've always found comforting. Maybe he knows I don't like people fussing over me and serving me meals, which is probably why they were never on any of my flights. I never need to eat or drink, and I can get my own blankets and such. Even when traveling on a commercial airline, I want be left alone. That's why I used to purchase two seats in first class, which seems pretty severe when I think about it now.

Baron and I stand in the aisle in a section where four reclining chairs face each other. I curve my neck to see through a slightly opened curtain. This is a huge jet, so this can't be the full scope of the seating area.

The two flight attendants are very pretty, and when they see Baron, they ogle him and turn giddy.

"Can I get you something?" the slight blond girl asks me as her eyes shift to Baron with that star-struck smile.

"Why don't you make yourself comfortable?" Baron holds out a hand, ushering me to sit before I can ask the girl if there's more seating in the back.

I slowly follow his suggestion as Baron ushers both flight attendants to the front of the airplane. I can't hear what he's whispering or thinking, but I can hear what they're thinking. They can't get over how *hot* he is, and they aren't sure if he and I are together. Then they're surprised that they don't have to work this flight after serving my meal, which is what he ordered. The tall one with long dark hair and olive skin is a little upset about not having to serve us because someone told her she's his type. I stand up to take off my coat; I'm not going anywhere now.

*Damn, look how he's looking at her*, one of the girls thinks.

I turn to see him watching me with narrowed, sultry eyes. I skip a breath.

"Anything else?" the disappointed girl asks him.

"No, that'll be all," he answers, not taking his eyes off me.

I sit back down. My head is spinning.

Soon we're all settled and trucking down the runway for takeoff. Baron took the seat across the aisle and diagonal from mine. He's reading through a thick report—which appears to require his complete attention—and one of the flight attendants has given me an e-reader with a stocked library.

Once the airplane is up and flying, I settle on *The Iliad* and *The Odyssey*. I read so fast that thirty minutes in, I'm almost done with *The Iliad*. I make a conscious effort to slow down a bit.

Baron says, "Greece," out of the blue.

I give him the obligatory pleasant smile. "Is that where we're going?"

"That's where we're going," he confirms.

"Thank you." I paste my eyes back on the screen, but I can feel that he's not done speaking to me yet.

"Are you hungry?"

I shake my head, refusing to look at him. "No, I told you earlier I'm not."

"But you have to eat, right?"

I look up at him. "*Why* are you trying to force me to eat?" I seriously don't get it.

"Because I… planned something that I think you'll like."

"Like what?" I still sound sort of brusque, but I want Baron to stop doing things that make me like him. We can never be friends.

Another thing I learned about men over the years is that they hate to be "the jerk." No decent guy—which most men are—wants to be the one to break a girl's heart. If they are the heart destroyer, then they loathe the idea of that girl hating them. The truth is, we'll get over it, but the guy has to go away, far away, so time can do its job. Baron Ze Feldis isn't going away, and he's behaving like a man who wants to eat both cakes when he's already chosen the one with butter cream frosting.

He seems unaffected by my tone because he hits the communication button and calls for my dinner. I'm still eyeing him suspiciously when a plate of berries, cream, and bread is carried out by the girl who thought she'd be a good match for him. I can't take my eyes off the food; it's plated beautifully. The cream and berries have been congealed somehow and are set on top of the flat bread. Thin lines of dark purple glaze cross the food. It's definitely from Enu, just gourmet-styled.

"Where did you get this?" I ask. I'd planned on holding out on food until we got back—if I made it back.

"I asked Fawn for it quite a while ago. It keeps really well."

"But why?"

I can see him thinking. I assume he doesn't want to reveal the reason, and if it stems from a time when we were together and he loved only me, then I don't want to hear it.

I lift a hand and say, "That's okay. You don't have to explain."

To my surprise, he allows that to be the end of it. As I eat, I have a couple of questions for him regarding our trip.

"Why would Lario be in Greece?" I ask.

Baron looks toward the entryway, through which the flight attendants disappeared. He gets up and slides another door shut.

"Soundproof," he explains as he takes his seat.

*My goodness, he's so tall and sexy.* I really want to have this conversation in his arms. Apparently that's reflected in my expression because he flashes that overconfident smirk again.

"There's a coven in Greece," he says.

"What kind of coven?"

"It's a community of vampires."

I take a moment to think it over. "Do you think it's safe for me there?"

"No, I don't. That's why you're staying in a hotel while I talk to some old acquaintances."

I snort, defiant. "I'm not staying in a hotel."

"I don't associate with any savage vampires, but even the politest vampire would kill me to drink your blood."

"Don't I have to give them permission?" I ask, raising an eyebrow. "Because I don't give them permission to drink my blood."

"They'll find a way to kill you and drink it. It's not hard to do."

"I could put an invisibility shield over myself. I've done it a lot, and it's ironclad."

He just nods. "Yes, but there's no need for you to do that. I'll go in, ask some questions, and if I get the information we need, we'll go see Lario."

"Ah." I finally understand what he's doing. He wants to be by my side right up until I face Lario. I shake my head, changing the subject abruptly. "What did you tell your mate?"

I know it's a sharp shift, but I have to ask. He's

planning to traipse around the globe with me if necessary, and I've seen how jealous vampire women can be.

He glares at me. If I didn't know him, it would be enough to make me tremble, but I know he'll never hurt me.

"I answer to no one," he says coldly.

"But isn't she worried? I would be," I press.

"Would you?" he snaps.

I frown, sensing there's a deeper meaning behind his sharp question. "Yes, I would be worried."

Baron's lips curl into a sinister smile. "Really? Even after being gone for two years? Then when you return, you head straight into a confrontation with Exgesis alone? Then you vanish for another year? Listen, Clarity… don't lecture me on being courteous to my mate. Out of the two of us, *I'm* the one who knows how to be properly in love."

My lips part in shock. For the first time, I see how angry he is with me. I never thought of it that way. Is there truly a proper way to be in a rela-tionship?

Until the day I met my first sister, I answered to no one but myself. I had no friends, and Freda, who I believed was my mother, wasn't much of one.

Felix, who I knew was my father, was hardly ever around. My relationships were with things like buildings and books and my work.

"I'm sorry," I mutter.

He keeps his eyes averted. "I've already forgiven you."

"Have you?"

He finally looks at me, and oddly enough, his gaze drifts over my body before returning to my face. He can't possibly be thinking about sex in a moment like this. "I have," he says, then returns to his reading.

I believe him, but I know he hasn't forgotten the pain I caused—just as I can't forget his. My goodness, I think we're truly done.

As soon as I finish my meal, Baron calls for the flight attendant to clear my plate.

"Bring the beverage," he says, glancing briefly at her.

I can feel her thoughts—she's wondering what I did to make him so upset, wishing he'd notice her, hoping for a sign of interest. She's ready to slip him a note inviting him to the back of the plane, where she imagines she could "make him happy."

"Yes, sir," she purrs seductively, but he barely notices.

He only looks up when I shift in my seat to gaze out the window. For a brief moment, his eyes sweep over me again. When the tea arrives, I turn back around, and I think his anger has passed because there's a smile on his face.

"Goshem tea?" I say, smiling back.

After making sure I'm content, he returns to his reading. I sip my tea and glance out the window. The plane is soaring over the Atlantic Ocean, nothing but darkness below us. The meal of berries, cream, and bread helps ease my anxiety about being alone with Baron. Slowly, I close my eyes and drift off to sleep.

Time passes, and I'm aware that I'm asleep. I feel warm all over and inside of me, as though I've had the perfect day. I see the light stirring in my head and feel a hand stroking my hip. My body is on fire, lit by passion. Whatever's happening, I'm ready to get fully involved with it. It's only when I caress my breasts that I slowly open my eyes to an embarrassing sight.

Baron is sitting directly across from me, watching me with narrowed eyes. I'm lying down because my seat and the one across from mine have been joined to make a bed. And I'm groping myself in front of him. *How embarrassing*.

"Are you comfortable?" he asks after swallowing hard. His deep eyes are ablaze.

I can't prove it, but I know he touched me. "I am."

We're staring at each other. Everything on my body that has a tip is standing firm.

"I like your dress," he says. "It looks good on you."

I look down at myself. Now I'm positive he touched me. "Thank you."

"You're welcome."

I smile at him because I'm sure I have nothing to be embarrassed about. I sit up. "So, do you like me in it enough that I can use it to convince you to take me to Vampire City with you?"

I haven't seen that naughty smirk of his in a long time. I wonder what thoughts are behind it.

He doesn't tell me, but he does say, "Yes, it's enough."

I hear myself giggling, which I never do, until I'm distracted by a cup of hot Goshem tea. I can see the steam snaking up from it.

"I wanted it to be warm when you woke up."

I frown at him. Maybe Lorenzo was right. We gave in to our sexual yearning for each other too quickly. Unlike my sisters, for whom I have a deep, ingrained commitment, I haven't learned to truly rely on Baron. Is he only irreplaceable to me on a sexual level? *I don't know*. But I'd take this over a roll in the hay any day.

"Thanks," I say as I sip my tea.

"You're welcome," he answers while studying his papers.

This is going to be the longest *short* trip ever.

## CHAPTER 4
# ENTER THE MOUNTAIN

The airplane lands at the perfect time of day, right after sundown. I do believe Baron planned it that way. For the rest of the flight, he'd read more of his papers, signing a few and drafting a few. He even asked if I thought Red Yard's brand contact plan targeted the right demographic.

"Remember that night?" he asked me. "The night you were supposed to pitch a plan to me at the Waldorf?"

I perch in my seat, boots off and curled up, grinning at him. "Yeah, the night I chickened out."

"Yeah, that night," he joked.

I chuckled.

"What would you have advised?"

I shrug. "I don't know. It was tough because Michael really didn't give me a historical report or anything. He didn't tell me what sort of person you were. Age…"

"But you knew me," he cut me off.

A scene from our night in Cambridge flashes in my mind. "I beg to differ. I didn't know you were a three-hundred-and-seventy-eight-year-old vampire."

I observed every inch of his face as he laughed. I thought I'd never hear him do that again. We went on to talk about advertising campaigns for Red Yard and Blue Tail, a new brand of beer he's on the verge of launching. I also learned that we were fellow alumni of Harvard Business School. He'd graduated in 1911 and then again in 1983, when all the people from the early days were good and gone.

So by the time we landed, it seemed it was too soon. I'm more confused than ever about who we were, what we are, and what we will become to each other in the future.

Baron instructs the flight attendants to stay in the main cabin until we deplane, and I create a shield of blindness over both of us. Taking refuge under the protection, we step out into the nippy evening. The cold goes right through my full-length winter coat. I'm already shivering, so Baron takes my hand. Of course I could spread a shield of warmth over myself, but I like this better. As soon as we touch, the cold fades away.

"Are you ready?" he's barely able to ask.

"I guess so." There's a tiny bit of trepidation in my voice.

"Relax, Clarity. I won't let anything happen to you."

I nod. Before our breakup, we would've kissed and turned the entire situation into a bed of roses. However, I'm realizing that I'm not as brave as I'd thought I was. So instead of holding his hand, I curl my arm around his waist and nudge my head into his chest. This stops my teeth from clattering with fear. Baron kisses my forehead, and I close my eyes to drink it in. *That's much better.*

We stand like this for a few moments until Baron asks, "Are you ready, love?"

I nod again and take his hand. I don't think he realizes he just called me "love," and I'm not going to point that out, especially since this moment feels like old times.

The next thing I know, we're riding the wind through the ancient city of Athens. I've traveled to Athens plenty of times on business. One of my clients was a Greek heiress who insisted we spend half of her advertising budget on connecting with consumers in the major Grecian outposts.

It's a modern city, and I do find it less religious in appearance than the rest of Europe. The other popular cities have Roman Catholic accents: circular domes, steeple rooftops, rounded windows, and bulging balconies. Basically everything looks to be only a cross and angel statue away from being a church. Athens is more classically designed. Its architecture is straight-lined and boxy—more governmental than religious. I always pay attention to the architecture when I travel; it tells me a lot about the values, beliefs, and mores of the society. This city is sprawling and compact—even in Manhattan, Americans couldn't live this close to each other.

We're in and out of Athens in a flash. Lyca-bettus Hill, rising like a shadow, is behind us. We cut through a forest, journeying into its pitch-black depths. Then Baron stops. We're standing very close to each other, our noses almost touching.

"I need you to make me visible," he whispers.

I swallow the lump in my throat before stepping back. I don't know if he meant to get that close to me, but his nearness sent my pulse racing. This is not the time to crave a kiss from Baron Ze Feldis.

"I did it," I say and swallow again.

"I'll need you to hop on my back and hold on."

I hesitate to examine our surroundings. We're standing among lofty trees. Their branches are thick and about thirty feet over our heads, adjoining to form lengthy canopies. That's why I can't see the sky. And that's why I step back toward Baron, who wraps his arms around me. One thing is for sure, I could never have come here alone or with anyone else, except for maybe Viesel Egos, who's been missing for a long time. It would be nice to have him and his sword of fire here with us.

"I'm not going to let anything happen to you," Baron assures me.

*Sometimes I think he can read my mind.* "Okay." My voice is shaky. "But where are we?" I glance over my shoulder.

"We're in the Agrafa Forest."

"Oh." I don't know why I say that. I think I'm trying to stall. "Are there vampires out here?"

"Hundreds."

I feel a chill go through my Life Blood.

"But a million vampires don't equate to the evil you fought at the gravesite, so you're afraid for no reason. You're brave." He cups my chin and lifts my face close to his.

I think he's going to kiss me, but if he does, we'll never stop.

"Get on my back," he whispers.

It takes a moment for him to let go of my face, but when he does, I climb on his back.

"Hold on tight because it can't seem as if I'm carrying you."

I wrap my arms around his neck and clamp my feet around his waist a little tighter, careful not to choke him.

"Tighter," he instructs me.

I increase my grip.

"That feels good," he says before taking off.

Nothing exists at this speed. It's so fast it actually feels as if we're not moving at all. We go deeper into the trees, and when he comes to a halt, we're at the base of a mountain. I begrudgingly slide off his back.

Before I can say a word, Baron presses his index finger over his lips, warning me to remain quiet. Just then, a feral growl echoes in the chilly air. Baron growls back but not as loud. Two guys—presumably vampires—dart out from the thick woods and flank him.

I'm standing right across from them. Both vampires have translucent, olive-toned skin that's severely chalky—I guess because they're Selells. They don't look alike, but they have similar high foreheads and long thin noses and faces. They remind me of subjects of classical sculptures, brought to life by the chisels of the masters.

"Is it you, Ze Feldis?" one of them asks, sniffing him like an animal.

"It's me."

"I smell something," the other one says. He sniffs in my direction.

I quickly create a veil of numbness, along with one of heat. I've been freezing since I let go of Baron's hand.

"Are you alone?" the first vampire asks. Even in the dark, I can see his shifty eyes searching through the brush.

Then the second vampire sniffs and sniffs until

his nose lands on Baron's shoulder. He grins. "Of course."

"Of course what?" Baron asks.

"I smell a woman on you."

"And she was as delicious as she smells," Baron replies, smirking at me.

I can't help but return the expression.

"Another human woman freely gives her blood to Baron Ze Feldis," the second vampire says facetiously. "As you can see, we're not so lucky."

"What the hell do you want?" the first vampire spits.

"I need to speak to Gia."

They shoot glances at each other.

"Is she here, Curtis?" Baron asks, a bit wary.

"No," the first vampire, whose name must be Curtis, answers.

"Then where is she?"

Again, they look at each other.

"Let's go inside. We've lingered long enough," Curtis says.

Baron stands still as the two men start off. They stop and look back at him.

"What are you waiting for?" the vampire who's not Curtis says.

I take that as clue to hop on Baron's back, and I do.

"I'm not," Baron says, and we shoot off.

We're moving so fast I can't see the world around me. However, I'm aware that we're no longer in the woods. We're rising toward the sky, and when we stop, we're on a steep cliff at the base of a stony mountain range. I want to ask Baron where we are, but I'm not that stupid. I've made them blind and numb to me, but why not deaf? I think *deaf* and visualize the scope of the veil.

"Baron, can you hear me?" I say in his ear.

His eyes expand with horror as he looks from face to face. It worked!

"I created a shield of deafness. You can hear me, but no one else can."

I attempt to slide off his back, but he reaches around to stop me. The two vampires are rolling a square block of rock from the mountain, exposing a narrow opening.

"Celeste is waiting for you," Curtis says.

Without delay, Baron darts through the entrance. The two vampires close the gap behind us, remaining outside. Baron finally takes his hands off my legs, giving me permission to slide off his back. Now that we're no longer touching, I feel empty inside.

Our steps are slow and careful. I study the place in awe. The rock walls on both sides of the narrow walkway look like ruins with thousands of tiny cubicles cut into the stone. Each opening has a tiny white light at the top center of it, and the thousands of lights give the place the dreariest feel. I almost regret coming here, but as I watch Baron's tall, strong figure, the regret goes away. I must confess I just want to be around him.

Loud hoots echo from the cubicles above, signaling Baron's arrival. He looks so out of place here. In his expensive heather gray trousers and freshly laundered black shirt, he's the man in a vodka ad campaign. He has a nice butt. This place was made for Indiana Jones. It could also be the set of one of those futuristic films where people are reduced to wearing potato sacks and having dirty faces. Every now and then, a head sticks out of one of the booths above us.

Suddenly a tall man with skin as dark as black licorice comes to a grinding halt in front of Baron. "Ze Feldis."

"Primoraen," Baron replies.

The whites of Primoraen's eyes are gleaming.

I've never seen anyone like him before. His skin is truly black. All of his features are slight—nose, lips, and chin—as if his face is disappearing right before my eyes.

"It's been a long time, Ze Feldis. You look… full."

Baron doesn't reply. He doesn't have to drink; he has me to keep him quenched.

"I'm looking for Gia," Baron says. "I need to ask her about Exgesis."

"You've certainly been out of touch with your *own* kind," Primoraen snarls.

Baron keeps his cool. "I'm a working man."

"More like a wealthy fat rat."

"Is she here or not?" His patience has worn thin.

Primoraen scowls. "Not."

"Then where the hell is she?"

"Dead," Primoraen says past clenched teeth.

Baron goes rigid. The way he flexes his jaw tells me he's disturbed by the news. I'm wondering why this Selell was so important to him when I'm rattled by a deafening, primal howl. Baron's face shoots upward. He catches sight of something. After a moment, his eyes sweep across my face, tipping me off that I should climb on his back. I'm not sure if

I'm imagining things or not, but it seems as if Primoraen is glaring right at me. His eyes are so maniacal that I tremble.

As soon as I hop on, Baron takes off toward the end of the corridor, which seems to be a half a mile long. We reach a mountain of stairs cut in the rock, and he doesn't slow down to mount them. Up, up, up we go, climbing high. We enter a domed corridor that holds red, blue, green, and orange lights, all coming together to create floating designs which swirl in the air. I feel as though we're in an art gallery, walking through a sci-fi-themed light installation.

I slide off Baron's back but take his forearm as we continue on. The truth is, I love touching him. He still smells good, and to be pressed against his back makes me feel as if I'm in heaven. He squeezes his arm into his side, trapping my fingers against him, and now I know what he thinks about my action.

We finally make another turn into an open-air area. It looks as if it's lit by natural light, which I know is impossible: first, it's night out; second, vampires can't live in the sun. So I look up to see what's causing this remarkable effect. Colored lights weave together, and their beams hit a single metal object, creating artificial sunlight.

"Oh my," I whisper, gazing at it.

"I knew you'd like it," Baron whispers very close to my ear.

The electricity of his mouth in such a sensitive area makes me whip my face around, and our lips are micro-inches away from touching. *Kiss me.*

Before he can possibly place his lips on mine, a huge voice sings, "He's back!"

Baron closes his eyes to take one deep sniff of my breath before turning. "Garrett!"

I let go of him so he can rush over to hug the vampire. I think it's funny that his name is simply *Garrett.* I mean, there's Lario Exgesis and Baron Ze Feldis, Primoraen. Yes, there was Curtis... but Garrett is so boy-who-lives-next-door-in-a-Midwestern-suburb.

"You look terrible, Ze Feldis. Absolutely disgusting," he says with an English accent.

"So do you," Baron bellows.

He's quite chipper. He grabs the guy again in a one-armed hug. I've never seen Baron this way. He's always so sober.

"I look thirsty, mate. But you know what they say…"

They both sing, "If I can't have blood, give me whiskey instead. Then give me the barmaid, and I'll take her to bed…"

"I drink by the barrel and shag every ten minutes!" Garret laughs.

Now that I'm able to study him closer, he does look intoxicated. I didn't think vampires could consume any food or drink.

"Come on," Garret hooks his arm around Baron's neck. "Celeste wants to see you."

I follow the two vampires just a little farther down the hall. When I look over the railing, I see where Garrett goes to guzzle his liquor and gather his women. Neon signs announce bars, advertising for vampires to come there and drink their thirst away. Not only that, but a humdrum beat slides through the air; it sounds like psychedelic rock.

The bar is nothing like a destroyed futuristic world where people have been reduced to living in rocks. Everyone dresses normally, and they're clean; the only thing they all are is thirsty—and probably drunk too.

Baron lets Garret step through an entryway blocked by another thick cloud of smoke, and then he lifts his arm for me to take. I hurry up and latch onto him. There's a steep slope I would've tripped down if I hadn't taken Baron's arm. On the leveled floor are cocktail tables and chairs occupied by smoking and drinking vampires. Each vampire eyes Baron for a second, but that's all. We weave through tables, walk behind the bar, and go through a door. We end up in a red-room lounge.

In a flash, a long, lean female who was stretched out on a red velvet round sofa in the middle of the room is up and only inches away from Baron's face. "Ze Feldis." She presses her lips against his for a kiss, but he doesn't kiss back. "No kiss?"

"Only for the ones we love," he says.

"Humph," she scoffs. "Is that your new motto? Because the Ze Feldis I know loves only this." She grabs his groin.

I almost gasp with shock, but he doesn't flinch.

He calmly removes her hand. "Every man changes."

"You are not a man; you are vampire." She has an accent; it sounds Bulgarian.

"Iva," calls a woman who appears behind her.

In one quick movement, Iva is back on the ottoman, lying on her side. Her eyes are narrowed to slits as she watches Baron seductively.

"Celeste," Baron says to the seemingly more mature vampire.

Her hair is strawberry blond and her skin translucent. She wears red lipstick, which makes her look even more washed-out. In man-years, she's probably not much older than I am, but I'm a freak of nature and divine. I've been filled out with curves since I was fifteen, and then my body stopped changing. I would like to go through some changes. There's a sexiness that comes with age, which Celeste manifests. She's very beautiful, and she has a demure quality that I haven't seen in this place yet.

"I know why you're here, Ze Feldis. Follow me," she says before turning and strutting across the floor.

Baron's glance signals me to follow. Iva twists to glare at him as we walk through another smoky doorway and into a private room with a huge bed and a table with two chairs. Baron and Celeste remain standing.

"You're looking for Exgesis," she says with one eye narrowed.

"Yes, I am. And Gia's dead?" There's still a hint of disbelief in his tone.

"She was drained by a vampire. Did you know vampires could do such a thing?"

Baron frowns while shaking his head. "No, I

didn't. How could that happen? Drinking another vampire is suicide."

"Not anymore, apparently. They're not dying; they're getting stronger."

"They?"

"There are packs of them," she says with spite.

Baron takes a moment to consider that. "Does Lario know Gia's dead?"

I want to tell him that if this Gia has been drained by another vampire, then Lario's the reason for it. I kick myself for missing the opportunity on the airplane to relay that information to Baron. I would tell him now, but it's not such a simple conversation. *I'll wait.*

"Ha! That bastard doesn't care about anyone but himself." Celeste drags her long figure over to a three-drawer chest to fish out a pack of cigarettes. "You cared about him. You were the only one who gave a shit about that snake in the swamp." She shakes a cigarette out of the container.

"I used to have nothing to hate him for."

"Is that what you think?" She dips the tip of the cigarette in a candle to light it and then greedily inhales.

Baron shrugs a shoulder. "Do you want to enlighten me?"

She blows smoke out of her mouth as she narrows her eyes at Baron. "You look like an angel, not the devil like the rest of us. Why are you not thirsty?"

Baron snarls. "Are you trying to insinuate I'm a murderer?"

"Are you?"

"No."

She takes another puff on the cigarette. "Last time I saw Exgesis, he was sniffing around the Shams."

"When was that?"

She makes a sudden move and stands nose to nose with him, petting his cheek. My mouth falls open. I can't believe how these vamp women are so easily coming on to him.

"Don't you know, Ze Feldis?"

"Know what?" Baron stands firm, unfazed by her.

"Not only is Exgesis a foul bastard, but he himself is a Sham."

"Exgesis practices magic?" Baron seems genuinely surprised to hear that.

Her hand falls to his chest as she unbuttons his shirt. "The darkest."

This time, I want to run out the room before I

have to see what she's trying to make happen. I sigh with relief when Baron grabs her wrists to stop her fingers.

"Which coven?" he asks.

"America only has one."

Baron gazes away. "Thank you." Now he's standing next to me.

She snorts a chuckle. "So it is true? I've heard the rumors."

He hesitates, eyeing her suspiciously. "What rumors?"

"About the Life Blood."

The rumbling growl returns to his throat.

"Look at you," she spits. "I know she's still alive because you're too in love with her. The old Ze Feldis would've thrown me on that bed."

In a swift move, his hand grabs her by the throat, choking her. "Will I have to kill you too?"

"No," she strains to answer, and he lets go of her. She steps far away from him, rubbing her neck. "It's not me you have to worry about."

"Then who?"

She shakes her head. "You can't kill them all."

"Who?"

She glares at him for a moment. "So this is Ze Feldis in love."

She's not happy about it.

"I'm jealous—*of the Life Blood, that is*," she says.

Baron makes a swift move, and they're nose to nose again. "You tell them—any of them—who come here looking for me that I *will* slice their heads off if they go hunting for the Life Blood."

His threat even gives *me* the chills, and I'm the one he apparently wants to save—and the one he *loves*?

"Come on, Ze Feldis," she pleads; lust colors her tone. "One more time." She nods toward the bed. "I've been waiting for you."

Baron makes another sudden move, and he's standing in front of me. I know it's time to get on his back.

"Good-bye, Celeste," he says.

"Never trust death, Ze Feldis. Dead or alive, Gia is not going to give up on you so easily."

Baron turns back to sneer at her—then to my relief, he speeds off and we're out of there.

## CHAPTER 5
# THE RESOLUTION

W e're soaring down the flight of stairs. Baron still seems pretty riled up from his conversation with Celeste. Truthfully, I am too. I know he loves me, but does he love me enough to reject the advances of two very sexy vampire women? Baron isn't a pig. He wouldn't bang them right there in front of me. But the way he rejected them—there wasn't even a hint of lust in his eyes. And what did she mean by Gia not giving up on him?

I'm so confused about what's going on between us when we arrive at the rock barricade. It rolls open, and Baron and I slip out. Never has the ice-cold night air felt so welcoming. He carries me at a remarkable speed down the mountain and back into the woods. I hate the dark woods, and Baron must feel me grab on tighter. When he comes to a stop, it's in an open-air gully enclosed by a thick line of tall conifers. The sky is congested with bulbous gray clouds; it looks as if it will storm at any moment. But something ominous lingers in the air.

"Keep me visible," Baron whispers. He must be able to feel it too. He peers deep into the trees.

I hear branches breaking and trees shaking. Primoraen and four others bolt out of the darkest part of the forest and surround us. If Baron's rattled in any way, I can't tell.

"Did you think we were just going to let you leave, Ze Feldis?"

Baron snarls. "Let me?"

"Where's the Life Blood? Is she here?" Primoraen turns his head this way and that, observing the emptiness. He must know I have the ability to be invisible, which is a lot to know about me.

"Let me pain them so we can get out of here," I plead, grabbing Baron's shoulder. I don't want him to fight; I just want to go. I don't even think he has his daggers.

In a swift movement, he takes my hand off of

his shoulder, squats down, and in a blink of an eye, stands, clutching a silver blade in each hand.

"I heard she enjoys saving you. Will she come for you this time?" Primoraen asks. His purple skin is so chalky that he looks scorched under the blackening sky.

I see the desperation in his eyes, the need to cure the thirst. "Don't. He's just thirsty."

"Five of us against your two blades. You've already lost," one of the other vampires hisses.

Baron does something between a snarl and smirk. The left side of his top teeth flashes. "She *would* beg me to spare your life. However, she doesn't know the treachery you're capable of, and I do." He grips his daggers tighter.

"It doesn't matter," I say.

Before I can continue in my effort to convince him to let them be, one of the other four vampires charges him. With one simple swipe, Baron takes off his head. It happened so fast, I couldn't scream. My mouth is stuck open. Blood gushes out of the sliced neck. This is going to get bloodier, and fast.

The others sway, probably trying to figure out if they should attack and what's the best way to do it. They know that Baron is much stronger than they are.

"Remember what Celeste said. It's common knowledge that I exist. If you kill them, there'll be more. We have to quench them, not kill them. You know this. You have the light, too!" That was my final stab at convincing Baron to retreat.

He glances at me. "Do it."

Without pause, I make him invisible. Then I make the four vampires numb to him. While they're looking at each other, confused and sniffing the air, I climb on his back. We get out of there.

---

WE'RE MOVING SO FAST THAT ALL I CAN DO IS CLOSE my eyes and press my face against his neck. Our speed cannot deaden the delicious scent of his skin. I nuzzle closer to him. I could ride like this all the way back over the Atlantic and into forever if time, or he, would allow it.

Instead of Manhattan, we end up in a European city. There are more bulky block buildings with domed or steeple roofs, rounded corners, lofty windows, and iron-barred balconies—another compact city with religious accents. Then out of nowhere, a contemporary skyscraper shoots into the sky. Still invisible, we enter one of the modern structures, a mirror-plated building. Baron gets us through the door so fast that the night guard doesn't even turn his head.

"Where are we?" I ask with a sigh of regret.

He slows to a walk, but I take one more whiff of his mint, lime, and black licorice scent before sliding off his back.

"Madrid," he replies once I'm on my own two feet.

"Wow! We've come a long way!"

It's unbelievable how fast he can travel. I must admit I'm a tad bit woozy—probably the human side of me.

"We have," he replies and takes my hand. "Let's get you rested."

There are now two night guards at the front desk. Security monitors are lined across a table in front of them, but the screen airing a soccer game claims their attention. Neither guard has a clue we just walked past them and down the hallway, rounding a corner.

Once we're in a private elevator, Baron touches a plate on the wall. As we're riding up to the sixtieth floor, I realize we're still holding hands. I let go of his. We're no longer lovers, and I want to make sure that he knows that I get it. He does crimp his brows a little, and once again I sorely wish to know his thoughts.

When the elevator doors slide open, he steps aside and waits for me to walk out. I see Baron look at my hand, and I think he wants to hold it again.

Instead of reaching for it, he says, "This way."

I follow him to what looks like the only door on the floor. After he pushes the door open and we walk in, the motion sensor lights cut on. Dim warm rays fall over über-fine furnishings—I mean *über fine*: intricately cut white velvet sofas, coffee and end tables, lamps, and shelves crafted with mahogany wood. What stands out is the triple-layer fireplace. As I study the build of it, flames burst out of the wood. Mirrors that are plated in the back and on the sides make it look as though a multitude of fires are burning into infinity.

"I knew you'd like it," Baron says. He's standing behind me. His energy tickles hot spots on my neck and back.

"It's very innovative." I also notice that there are no windows. Walls built of white granite are erected where glass should be.

"Come, I'll show you to your bed."

I follow him down another long hallway with a high-arched ceiling; scenes of Spanish culture are hand-painted on the plaster. I look up to view a matador teasing a bull with his red cape and flamenco dancers fanning their skirts and curving their swanlike necks.

"Here," Baron says, ushering me toward a room.

I tear my eyes away from the ceiling. Red silk sheets adorn a large poster bed that's so high off the ground there's a wooden step stool beside it. I turn to meet his eyes. "It's official. You have exquisite taste."

I know we both are stalling. The moment is awkward. Do we or don't we sleep together? So I walk in and, without using the step stool, lift myself onto the edge of the bed. Baron stands on the threshold. I pat the empty spot beside me. He doesn't bolt across the mahogany hardwood floor but takes his time walking over. His eyes pick me apart. I feel myself skipping a breath, which is a complete mistake. I'm trying to contain the sensations being close to him stirs up in me, especially in this sort of situation.

I turn to look at him. "So I have to tell you something." I take a deep breath and let it out slowly. "When Lario was changed back into a vampire, he was changed into a type that can drink from other vampires."

Baron's expression is unreadable. He stares into my face as if he's stunned. I think he's reflecting on this revelation that I waited much too long to tell him.

"Not only that," I continue, "but according to the Script, he's using magic against the power of the mind. Right now, he's looking for a vampire with the power of the sun."

"You're telling me this now?" he says.

"I know," I say with a sigh. "It's only when we were in the mountain that it hit me that I can't do this without you. When Celeste mentioned vampires drinking vampires, I thought 'Stupid me! I should've told you that already.'" I hang my head, overdoing the self-deprecation.

He lifts my chin. "It's okay, Clarity. I understand."

We let the silence settle for a few seconds.

"So when you find Exgesis, what is it that you want from him?" he asks.

"I need to find the power of the sun before he does. I tried to find him and stick with him by using my ability, but he's found a way to fight me. I can't get near him."

"Ah, I see. He's using magic."

"According to the Script, he's using magic, but I never would've guessed that he's the actual sorcerer."

"I wouldn't either. But I'm not surprised," Baron spits.

"No?"

"I knew Exgesis when he was human the first time."

My jaw drops. They've must've known each other for a very long time.

"He'd come to a tavern that I owned in Naples. Zina ran the bar," he continues, peeking at me.

The last time I saw Zina, her head was flying past me after Baron sliced it off, seconds after she stabbed me through the back.

"Zina would seduce, and we would drink." He frowns. "But Lario knew what we were the second he walked through the door. He also knew he wanted to become a vampire. I turned him down, but Zina didn't. Not because she planned to go through with it—she was just as cunning as he was," he snarls. "Lario already knew that if he said stop at any point while Zina drank him, she would have to comply."

"That's a lot for a human to know."

"Yes, it was."

"So how did he become a vampire?"

"There has to be an exchange of blood. The vampire is only allowed to drink from the body of a human, but the human doesn't have to drink from the body of the vampire. Exgesis convinced Zina to fill a goblet with her blood. She was so thirsty that she didn't question him. When she sank her teeth into him, before he could pass out, he told her to stop. From downstairs, I heard her scream, 'You tricked me!' While she was hysterical, Lario downed the goblet of blood and stabbed himself in the heart. Thirteen days later, he was a vampire."

"He not only knew what he wanted, he knew exactly how to get it," I conclude.

"Right. And no other vampire would tell him that. We don't want anything from a human but their blood, and giving them the secrets to stop us from getting it is… counterproductive."

"Do you think he used magic to learn everything about vampires?"

Baron lifts his eyebrows, as if what he's about to reveal will knock my socks off. "No human sorcerer can conjure magic that strong. Just like Sham magic can't stop you from tracking Exgesis. He's using magic, but it's not his own."

"Or human or vampire?"

"No."

"Then what?"

"A much stronger power. One that could only battle the kind of power that supports you and know your power's deepest, darkest secrets because it was there from the beginning."

"The Evil?" My chest and throat are tight. I hug myself to soothe the fear running through me. "I still don't understand how."

"It doesn't matter."

"It doesn't?" I'm so mesmerized by his nearness it has momentarily quashed my fear. *Get a grip*. I was so caught up in the story that I forgot Baron and I were alone on a bed.

"No, it doesn't." He doesn't stop searching my eyes.

*What is he looking for?*

"I was angry at you for three years," he says, completely changing the subject.

I sigh. "I know; I read that loud and clear on the airplane."

"I still am," he admits.

"I read that too. But…" I've always subscribed to listening to the other person and not sharing the blame with the blamer. I, the woman with a thousand rules of communication, am somehow the worst communicator in the world when it comes to him.

"But?"

"Never mind." I wave dismissively.

"You can say it, Clarity. Please say something," he pleads.

I swallow hard, wondering what I am afraid of. Maybe further alienating him? "Well… the first two years were out of my control. I left Enu as soon as I could."

"But you didn't come to me."

"No. Fawn was in trouble."

"But you didn't think I could help?" he asks.

"I wasn't thinking."

"You shouldn't have had to."

I shake my head. "I don't agree."

"I know." He shoots to his feet. "There's a bathroom around the corner. You can put your clothes in the chute, and they'll be cleaned for you by the time you wake up. Rest well; we'll leave at sundown."

I nod stiffly. I want to cry, but I fight the impulse with every fiber of my being.

He studies me closely as if he's waiting for my rebuttal. The only problem is I don't have one.

*Maybe he's right.* I'm not the sort of female who has to rustle up a man every time she's in trouble, but if I'm properly in love, then maybe that's supposed to be who I become. I don't know. I want to be everything he needs me to be, but I don't want to lose myself in the process. I'm still so very confused, and I need time alone to think.

"We're going to where the North American Shams are" he says before he practically disappears.

I take off my coat and boots before dragging myself to the bathroom. After stripping out of my dress and underwear, I follow Baron's instruction and drop them in the chute. There's a European-style bathtub with a golden-clawed foot at each corner. I fill the tub and add bath milk and bubbles. Once it's ready, I step inside and close my eyes. It's so comfortable that instead of thinking of *something*, I can only think of *nothing*.

A short catnap later, I get out of the tub, dry off, and slip between the sheets. Once I'm all settled between the covers, the lights turn off. In the dark, I wonder if Baron is asleep. He can sleep now that he's no longer thirsty. Just when I decide to doze off, there's a light knock on the door. I'm sort of spastic as I sit up. The motion light clicks on.

"Who is it?" I ask but then realize it could only be one person.

"It's me," Baron quietly answers.

I twist and turn all over the place, searching for that stunning kimono bathrobe that was hanging in the dressing room. But I can't find it. The only thing I see to cover myself with is my trench coat. I leap off the high bed, snatch it off a red suede armchair, and slide into it.

"Yeah?" I say too loudly as I crack open the door.

His eyes fall to my chest. I follow them to see what's causing that reaction.

"Oh." I pull the jacket across my exposed cleavage.

Even though I'm covered, Baron is still staring as if he can see right through the material, which I know he cannot.

"Did you want something?" I ask, frowning.

He takes my hand and moves it away from where I've been clamping the jacket closed. I don't think I can breathe as lust shines in his eyes. He presses a finger against my hard nipple, making every sensitive part of me throb, and then he lowers his mouth to it.

Now it's very clear why he knocked on the door.

"I want you, Clarity," he says as he pulls my jacket open and off.

I'm completely nude, and he stands back to get an eyeful before he snarls with desire. Before I know it, I'm lying on the bed, and his mouth is everywhere—my nipples, neck, back to my nipples, abdomen, pelvis. Then his lips kiss down to a place where he stays, and stays, and stays. I moan and squirm, almost unable to take it until I cry out in sheer pleasure. Instead of stopping there, he shifts his tongue a little, and a few seconds later, I cry out again. He does this over and over and doesn't stop until he gets what he wants, which is me in a state of frenzy.

Finally, he tears his expensive shirt open, buttons and all, slips out of his pants, and slowly, almost ceremoniously, slides inside of me. At first, he's very still, staring into my eyes. "I love you."

"I love you too," I whisper. It's as if a boatload of bricks have tumbled off my shoulders.

"I will never stop loving you."

"Me neither."

He presses his lips to mine. Our mouths are warm; the kiss is soft. He pulls back to look at my face, then he lowers his mouth to kiss my top lip.

When I try to kiss him back, he whispers, "No. Please."

"What?" I'm shocked that he is so controlled.

"I've been waiting three years for this. It's hard to contain myself."

"You don't have to." I cup my hands around his chin.

He turns toward my left palm and kisses it. Very carefully, he thrusts again. When he does that, I can't help but moan. We merge deeper into each other. He too allows a whimper to escape. The moment I cry out, he lets go, and his throaty, animalistic growl bounces off the walls.

We do this over and over, making up for lost time. My tolerance for the magnitude of the pleasure making love to him brings me has increased. But finally I can't take anymore, and after one last cry and growl of passion, we lie side by side, staring into each other's eyes.

"What does this mean? Are you and I together again?" My eyelids are heavy; I could sleep for a week.

He hums thoughtfully. "That night you told me to meet you in Manhattan, I showed up at your apartment. Even the next night and the night after that. Six months, at sundown, I went there. But you never showed. I felt like I'd been punched in the gut. I felt you when you returned a year later, but…"

"But I had already broken your heart." I never wanted to hurt him, and I wish I could do it all over again. I'd do things differently, that's for sure.

"Yeah," he says as if he's reliving the pain. "I was angry with you."

"I know. I thought we were solid, so I stayed until Fawn woke up."

"How could you think we were solid when you'd been gone so long? It drove me crazy not having you here. I excused the first two years, I really did. You were… you were close to death when I had to leave you in Egos's hands. But the second time… it just confirmed the lie Exgesis told me. I arrived at a million conclusions before I believed that you'd only wanted to meet me at your apartment so you could tell me you're with Egos."

"You mean the man who never talks?" I scoff, wondering how he could ever believe that. "That almost feels incestuous."

He frowns hard. "Is that so?

"Yes, it is so."

"Well, I believed the lies."

"I understand." The sensor turns off the lights. "I've never been in a relationship before, and I guess you needed some sort of reassurance." I sigh hard. "It never occurred to me that you were hurt. I thought you'd left me because you were trying to protect me. I can't read your mind, and I got it wrong."

"I will always protect you," he says as he pulls me into him. The lights turn back on.

"I know."

After a long moment, he asks, "Do you think the Wek was right?"

"About me and you and sex?"

"I do want to make love to you again, see?" He guides my hand to his brand-new erection. Then he slides a finger through my wetness. "And you want me, I see." He smirks, making me want him even more.

"Every time I'm near you, I want you. It's like I have to merge into your soul or something," I confess.

"Same here."

"It didn't feel like this with the one human I had sex with."

"Just one?"

"Only one. I did it with him because I wanted to get it over with."

"But you're so sexy."

"Believe me, I heard that over and over again, but…" I try to think of how to say that knowing what another person is thinking and feeling doesn't make me feel sexy. "It was just never that important to me."

"Well, it's no secret that I've had sex with humans and vampires, and it *never* felt like this. I can hardly contain myself when I'm inside of you."

I leer at him seductively. "And I can hardly take it. But…"

"But?"

"But I think we can get lost in this. I mean, I thought I'd convinced you that I'll never leave you for anyone, but I didn't. We have to live being in love for a while, build a long run—that's all." I smooth his eyebrows. "So… are we back together?"

"Hell yes," he says.

He mounts me. I open my legs for him, and Baron indulgently slips inside my wetness, groaning at his first thrust. We make love slowly and deeply, hoping it'll last forever.

It may be negligent on both of our parts, but Lario will just have to wait. Time goes by. We lie in each other's arms, unable to keep our hands off each other. I'm never satiated and neither is he; there's no bottom. And we talk about so much during our breaks.

"We can live anywhere in the world," he says, sounding so sure.

"But you work in New York."

"I don't work anywhere. I buy companies, make them better, and then sell them."

"But you're involved in ad campaigns."

He gives me that crooked smile. "Well, I did all that for you."

"But I haven't worked at the firm in years."

"I know. But you're in advertising. I counted on you returning one day."

"Was," I correct him. "I was in advertising. I'm never going back there."

"So where are you taking me?" he asks jokingly. We grin at each other.

I hum, as I exaggerate thinking. "Stars Hollow."

"Where's that?"

"*Gilmore Girls.*"

"What's *Gilmore Girls*?"

I chuckle. "It's a TV show."

"You're taking me to a TV show?"

"No," I whine, free and cute-like. I can't believe I feel like this. I'm not the giddy type. "A place like Stars Hollow. I'll be Ms. Patty, and you can be Luke Danes."

He frowns so very confused. "Who's Luke Danes?"

I chuckle again. "He owns the diner."

"And who's Ms. Patty?"

"She owns the dance studio, but she's an actress. She sings and works with the kids."

He grunts thoughtfully.

"What?"

"You want to have children?"

I think about it again. "No, I don't. But I like kids. Their minds are so… unsullied by the world. They're always so confused by adults. I just want to make it all make sense to them, you know? Be their *Catcher in the Rye*."

Baron takes my hand and folds his fingers into mine. "Done. We'll live in Stars Hollow. I'll buy myself a diner, and we'll get you a dance studio. And I'll bet you children will show up as soon as they hear about the beautiful new dance teacher in town."

I laugh. "Yeah, but Baron's Diner can only be

open at night. I mean, you *are* a vampire."

"Ah, yes, that." He nods.

"But"—I lift a finger to mark my point—"we can go to Rory's birthday party. October 31$^{st}$, Halloween. The perfect night for vampires."

He laughs. I'll never stop loving his laugh. Then the next thing I know, he's on top of me again. Our lips melt together. I love how he singles out my top lip, then bottom lip, and then goes in for my tongue. He's a skillful kisser, which makes me an even better kisser. Each time we make love is different than the last. Every time the lights cut on and off, we laugh a little.

"Didn't expect to do this in here?" I ask with a little chuckle. Probably five hours have passed since our last conversation.

"No, actually, I didn't."

Then I remember the female vampires and how easily they groped him and kissed him. I start a new conversation, wanting him to address what that was all about.

"I've lived a long time without you," he says. "But I really didn't want you to see that. I haven't been that way for a long time. I changed before I met you."

I run my finger down the tip of his nose and then his cheek. How can someone be so beautiful and sexy at the same time? It's unfair to be blessed with both attributes.

I can see how my touch causes him to skip a breath, but his lust disappears when I ask, "Who's Gia?"

Baron stares at the ceiling. "She's someone Lario and I fell in love with at same time. She chose Exgesis."

"Over you?" I ask in disbelief. That just doesn't make sense.

"He's a charming guy."

"He's annoying," I counter, "and so cavalier I could hardly stand it."

Baron faces me. "She was the only person Exgesis ever loved. And you're the only person I have *truly* ever loved."

"So he didn't love Fawn?"

Baron hesitates. I think he wants to be careful, knowing how much I love my sister. "Let's just say his actions speak louder than his words, don't they?"

I swallow a hard lump of hate and nod stiffly.

"When Gia finally told me she loved me, it was too late."

"Because of me?"

"It was a hundred years ago, so no…" He smiles. "It was because deep down, I knew."

"Knew what?"

"This…."

We're kissing again, our bodies and souls struggling to merge into one. I know a lot of time is passing. During our downtime, we plan our future vacations and think of quaint little towns to live in while we let the world pass us by. We do fit in a little sleep.

We're making out and rolling over the messy red sheets when I hear, *Cl'auta, it's time.*

I sigh and say, "The Wek calleth."

We do it one more time before I get in the shower. Baron goes to collect my clean clothes before joining me. I decide not to even ask how he did that. All of my life, I've lived in places where chores mysteriously got done. He watches me slip on my underwear and dress; I can see he wants to take it all back off.

"Maybe you should wait in the living room or somewhere," I suggest.

He laughs a little. "I think I should. I've needed to touch you since I first saw that dress on you. But

I'll wait until later to take it off of you." Baron winks, and then in a flash, he's out of the room.

———

ALTHOUGH LORENZO WAS IN MY HEAD, HE NEVER showed up. He's watching, I guess. But after we ride the elevator down and enter the lobby, there's an old friend waiting for us at the door.

CHAPTER 6

# THE BLACK HILLS

Viesel Egos stands at the glass sliding doors. Those intense blue eyes are still piercing. Two men in suits stomp through the lobby, both leaving for the evening; neither one notices the ominous-looking man standing right in the middle of the doorway. They avoid colliding into him only by a few inches. Even though Baron undoubtedly knows I have no romantic feelings for Viesel Egos, the corners of his mouth turn down.

"Hi, Viesel Egos," I say. I can't help but grin; it's nice to see him. If he were human or even Enuian, I would hug him, but my instincts tell me that Viesel Egos doesn't do hugs or handshakes.

He doesn't return my salutation. Instead, he heads out the doors. We follow him out of the building, and he pulls the car door open for us. I figure that's his greeting, since the doors of the cars he drives usually open on their own. Once we're inside, he zooms away.

Riding through the streets gives me a better sense of how antiquated this city really is. We're moving down streets lined with buildings that could easily be joined with their neighbors to form one city-wide cathedral. After the first five trips to this part of the world, it gets monotonous.

I decide to focus on what's inside the car. Baron's hands are pressed against his lap, so I take one of his.

"We're on our way to my jet, I assume?" Baron asks Viesel Egos.

Only now do I hear how tense he is.

"Yes," Viesel Egos replies.

Baron relaxes the grip on my hand. I think he's satisfied by that response.

"I wonder how long we've been off the radar," I say.

"Four days," Baron replies.

"Really? That means it's…"

"Sunday."

"Oh." I'm embarrassed. Clarity Parker doesn't make love, catnap, and waste precious time fantasizing about a future that can never be as long as things are the way they are.

Lario's new breed of vampires could've wiped the old breed off the face of the Earth in four days. He's probably already found and started torturing the vampire with the power of the sun. I look at my lap to avoid seeing Viesel Egos's eyes, though he's not looking at me. Baron gently takes my chin, lifts my face, and kisses my lips.

"It's okay, Clarity." His voice is soothing.

"What? I didn't say anything." I come off jittery. I force myself to smile, pretending not to feel so ashamed of myself.

"You don't have to." He grins.

I sigh, relieved that I don't have to put on a strong face. At the moment, I'm probably the most confused person on Earth. I feel as if I showed up too late for a proctored exam and have been asked by the professor to leave. "And you'll receive a 'fail,' Ms. Parker," this made-up professor says. That's never happened to me, of course, because I'm always on time and soaring far above top-notch. Now I hate Lario, and needing to stop him is changing me; I don't know if it's for the better.

We board Baron's jet at a small airport. Viesel

Egos remains behind the wheel of the car after my door flies open.

"You're not coming?" I ask him while hanging halfway out of the back seat.

"I'll be there when I'm needed," he says, as robotic as usual.

"Okay." I give up on treating him like a human —or anything more than a robot.

Before I can fully step out of the car, he says, "Cl'auta."

"Yes?"

"I'm glad you recovered."

"Thank you." I'm shocked.

Then he puts those fiery eyes on Baron, who's waiting for me by the ramp. "Tell Ze Feldis thank you."

"But he was right here," I say, insinuating that he should've told him himself. I'm messing with him, like old times.

Viesel Egos glares at me. I can't help but grin. It's been too long since I've frustrated him to that point. He's like a big, brooding brother, one who's fun to dig at.

The two female flight attendants are back and still hoping for a taste of Baron. One girl even has her cleavage pushed up and out for him to ogle.

Can't blame them for trying. He is a stunning being. I should be a little more jealous, but I'm not. That emotion has eluded me all of my life. I can thank my ability for that.

"Hope you enjoyed your trip," Cleavage Girl says to Baron.

"We did." He smirks at me.

I chuckle and shake my head at him, reading his hidden meaning. This time he prepares to sit directly across from me. I take off my coat and boots, and Baron puts them in the closet for me. He tells the flight attendants to provide minimal service again and settles into the comfy leather chair.

"Ready to join the Mile High Club?" he jokes.

I laugh. We beam at each other as the airplane trucks down the lanes to line up for take-off. There's no doubt what's on his mind. We break eye contact when a butterfly flies in through the metal walls and clings to a seat across the aisle. We're not shocked when Lorenzo materializes.

"What are your plans?" he demands, staring at me.

I get the feeling he's agitated by something, possibly the fact that Baron and I took time off to "officially" make up. The takeoff light blinks on the arm of my chair, and the jet races down the runway. I brace myself as we go up.

"I've learned Lario is a Sham," Baron answers in my stead.

"A sorcerer," Lorenzo reflects. "Human Shams or vampire?"

"Vampire," Baron answers.

"I know where to find every human Sham in existence, but the vampires change covens frequently," Lorenzo remarks.

Baron nestles deeper into his seat. "But I know where they are." He sounds very confident.

"How?"

Baron leans on his armrest and squeezes his lips. He's apprehensive, and I'm curious about why that is.

"Tal," he says and focuses on me. "You saw her."

After a moment, I ask, "That night at the Met?" I feel my head floating away from my body.

He nods. "She's a Sham." His lips tighten a bit. "I should've known she was tethered to Exgesis."

"You think?" I sound a little miffed because I am. I'm infuriated with Lario, though, not Baron. This is just another reason why Lario needs to die.

QUENCHED

"Tal and I never consummated a bond," Baron says in his defense. "One, because I loved you, and two, because I could never trust her."

"How did you meet her?" I ask.

He looks at me really hard, and I keep my expression open. I know he's testing me, seeing if I really want to know the answer. I hope he sees that I do.

"She showed up at a Red Yard event. We talked for a while." His brows knit together. "I wasn't in the best frame of mind then, but I recall being sort of alarmed when she mentioned that I had a broken heart. I hadn't told her anything about… what happened between you and me."

I scowl. "Lario told her, I bet."

"I'm sure of it. She had been winning me over up until that night. When I saw you. She always said the right things."

"But you said you were bonded to her."

He sighs. "I was angry with you. I wanted to say something to make you feel like… me."

"So you're not bonded to her?" I ask.

"No, I'm not."

"You lied?"

"Yes, I lied. But I'll never lie to you again."

"I know."

"But while we were dancing," he continues, "she whispered that she wanted to make my night as magical as the Shams of the Black Hills would. It didn't mean anything to me until Celeste told me Exgesis is a Sham."

"What could he gain by…" Then it hits me. "You wield the light. He had to have known that about you from Day One. That's why he's looking for this other vampire. You have the power of light, and this other vampire has the power of the sun."

"And you were the one who ignited it in me."

My heart drops. "One of my sisters has to ignite the power in this other vampire."

"I heard you say you didn't swear yourself to this Sham," Lorenzo says. "Did she swear herself to you?"

After a moment, Baron nods. He avoids looking at me. I know what that means. Like Zina, Tal drank a drop of his blood.

"May I touch your mind?" Lorenzo asks.

Baron glances at me. "Of course."

Lorenzo stands in front of Baron and presses his hands on Baron's temples. It's only a couple of seconds before Lorenzo steps away. "Cl'auta, Ze Feldis, I'll see what I can discover."

He transforms into the butterfly, and we watch him fly through the wall. Baron stares at me again but not in the seductive I-want-to-snatch-your-clothes-off-and-make-love-to-you way. He's wondering how much damage he's done by revealing the full truth about Tal.

To put him at ease, I muster the warmest smile I can. "That's in the past, Baron. We're in the present, and we have the future."

The next thing I know, I'm sitting in his lap. His hands slide up and down my torso.

"I'm cheating," he says before kissing my neck.

"What do you mean?" I whisper, skipping a breath.

"I'm supposed to wait to *ceremoniously* take this dress off of you."

I chuckle. "I rather wait for the ceremony, then."

"Me too," he says.

We kiss deeply until, with another swift movement, I'm back in my seat. I laugh once. "I'm impressed by your ability to do that."

"Do you want me to do it again?" he jokes.

"No," I say, still smiling. "Plus, I just thought of something."

"Thought of what?"

He's serious again, which makes me turn serious. He validates all of my thoughts, as if whatever I conjure up is extremely important. *Gosh, I love that about him.*

"Do you think Lario is using magic on humans to influence their will?"

"No. He can't." He sounds sure. "But you'd be surprised how often humans seek out vampire Shams. Shams trade their magic for a drink from the human. They just don't drink them dry."

"Why not?"

"It's good business not to kill the customer."

"What about changing the customer into a vampire?"

A flash of intuition causes Baron to lift his eyebrows. "It's a possibility. Exgesis could definitely use his Sham influence to get humans to turn themselves into vampires. When they come to him, they've already sacrificed their will."

I have a lot to think about as the flight attendant sets a tray of the same cuisine I'd eaten on the trip over in front of me. She's given up on getting Baron's attention because she made the mistake of taking his rejection as confirmation that I'm "hotter" than she is. I found myself wanting to correct her misconception of the facts. The truth is, he's a decent being who knows how—as he says—to properly be in love, *and that's with me.*

"What are you smiling about?" he asks.

"I'm keeping *that* to myself." I wink at him.

He winks back and doesn't push for an answer. I love that about him too.

As we fly back over the Atlantic Ocean, Baron takes a whole host of business calls. He even has a call with Michael Colton, who must've asked about me because Baron says, "she's here with me." Then Michael must say something Baron doesn't like because he frowns. It's clear from his reactions that Michael keeps talking about me. I'd always thought Michael had a crush on me. I put a lot of effort into staying out of his head because he was my boss.

Baron says, "Yes, we're together," and then, "Yes, we're *together* together."

Baron frowns so hard it looks as if he's just eaten a lemon, but he does manage to wink at me. I laugh a little.

As I sip on Goshem tea, I ponder what he just declared to someone who's part of the real world. I'm actually the other half of a *couple*. I never thought that day would come. I was never made for human men. Yes, I was always meant for a supernatural creature. I was always meant for Baron Ze Feldis.

I don't know when, but I fell asleep in my chair. At some point, I feel myself laid out in a proper sleeping position. I want to thank Baron for transforming the chair into a bed for me, but my eyelids are too heavy. And then a hard body presses against my back, and I know I'm no longer sleeping alone.

---

WHEN I WAKE UP, THE PLANE HAS ALREADY LANDED in Gillette, Wyoming. Baron warns me that it's icy cold outside, and my dress and boots will not keep me warm for very long if he lets go of my hand.

"I can put a shield of warmth over me," I confess. "I just let you hold my hand in Greece because I wanted you to."

He lets me hear that intoxicating chuckle of his, and once again, I'm mesmerized by the sound of it. Before we move out of the airplane, I initiate my veils: warmth, blindness, numbness. I am prepared to use others if need be. Once again, the flight attendants remain in the back section of the airplane as we exit. Stepping out into the night, I can sense the Evil is not too far away.

If it weren't for the snow glistening over everything—tree branches, the fields, the rooftop of the airport—it would be a lot darker. It's nothing like how it looks when snow falls on Central Park or the cherry blossom trees in the smaller parks of Manhattan, or how the vapory clouds that bring us the icy rain swallows up the tops of lofty skyscrapers. Normally I would straighten my back and put on the appearance of courage, but with Baron Ze Feldis, I need to conjure no pretenses. I take hold of his arm while trembling.

He looks down at me, concerned. "I thought you had a veil of warmth."

"I do," I admit.

He pulls me in his arms and looks me in the eye.

"I think I'm afraid *again*," I admit.

After searching my eyes, he says, "I can feel it too. And you fought this before. We fought it. So don't be afraid of it. It thrives off of fear. You know that already."

He's still holding me tight, refusing to let go until he sees that I get it. I'm trying to "get it." I remember the trees bending as the Evil chased me to Enu. And then our fight at the gravesite. How the black shadows and skeletal faces, all unique, live inside of it. Death is what the Evil is. Death that's still alive.

On the other hand, I see myself lifting my palm toward that ruthless force and prevailing against it. I came out with the Script. But I'm not a surface thinker. I'm a deep thinker, and that's why doubts spring up. I consider the fact that the Evil must've been in cahoots with Lario even then. Maybe it *allowed* me to secure the Script because it thought it would end up in Lario's hands. If I fight it today, then it has no motivation to go easy on me. We'll be engaged in an all-out war.

"Are you ready now?" Baron asks. He still looks as if he's not sure that I'm calm enough to move forward.

I put on the bravest face I can muster. There's no going back, no retreating. "I'm ready." I force myself to sound resolute.

Baron nods. "It's best to go at your speed. The Shams can feel the wind of the vampire's swiftness."

I gulp. "Lead us on." I sound too chipper.

Baron frowns. I think he's detected my false sense of bravery.

"You're going to be fine," he reassures me before taking my hand. "You'll see."

And off we go across the ice and past the conifers. The trees rise like a trillion black giants. They not only paint the valleys but the mountain ranges too. I definitely see where the Black Hills gets its name. I'm pulling energy from the entire span of the landscape, and that's when I hear their minds, hundreds of them. We are far from being alone.

"Stop," I whisper. "There are vampires here. Lots of them."

Out of nowhere, Viesel Egos appears right beside me, opposite of Baron. My heartbeat recovers from being startled.

"Viesel," I say with relief.

He glances at me quickly, his hand in his jacket. More than likely, he's clutching that flaming sword of his. He and Baron glance at each other, confirming they're in agreement. For sure, they're both ready to fight.

But my instincts are telling me that now is not the time for physical battle. Without warning, Baron grabs his ears and grunts in severe pain. Thinking fast, I let my mind build a thick, impenetrable shield around his ears.

I sigh with relief when he drops his hand. He pants as the pain subsides. By how he's snarling, he's enraged by what just happened to him.

"They know we're here. We have to get closer," Baron growls past clenched teeth. His eyes shoot daggers across at the edge of the black mountain.

But just before he can take off, I grab his arm. "Wait, that's what they want."

"That's what they'll get."

Even Viesel Egos has his sword in hand, ready to fire it up.

But I stand firm. "Listen, I think we should do the opposite of what's expected."

Baron frowns at me while Viesel Egos glares at the Black Hills. His eyes shift from spot to spot. I'm positive he can see each and every one of the vampires dug into the trees on the mountains.

"Lario thinks I've given up on traveling out of myself to get to him. I think he thinks he's outsmarting us. Let's use the power of light to get me close to him," I suggest.

We're standing amongst the spikes of tall evergreens. Just ahead, a gully of pure white snow goes on for about a quarter of a mile before the tree-line starts and flows up the foothills. Baron is obviously itching to wield those daggers. He still hasn't forgiven the Sham who hit him with that piercing noise.

"Hey, if this doesn't work, then we'll give it all we got and take them on," I promise.

Baron and Viesel Egos nod at each other. Without speaking, Baron stuffs the daggers back in the holsters wrapped around his ankles and holds out his hands, offering access to his light. I sigh with relief as I weave my fingers between his and press our palms together.

The light rushes into me but doesn't jolt me. It infuses me with a warmth so deep I feel it from the tips of my toes to the crown of my head. I can actually differentiate between the rays that fill Baron and my own. Our lights swirl around each other faster and faster until they become one. I'm ready to take all that I can handle.

I picture Lario's face, his very tan, almost orange skin punctuated by a full head of white hair. I see those dark eyes of his and hear him say, as superior as always, "You got no choice, Johnny."

I'm in a room. There's a bed with messed-up sheets, a scratched old dresser drawer against the wall, syringes and towels stained with dried blood on top of the drawer, and then *Johnny's* slumped on the side of the bed. Johnny's a *she*, not a *he*. She's a very beautiful coffee-colored girl with a cropped haircut, heart-shaped face, and doe eyes. She's wearing a tight yellow mini-skirt that illuminates her brown skin, a green-and-yellow striped halter top, and black thigh-high patent leather boots. She's dressed to party and have a good time, but the poor girl looks as if the weight of the entire world has just crashed down upon her.

"I just want to go home," she whimpers.

Lario stands above her, lording over her. It's his way of showing her who's in charge. "*You.*" He emphasizes that word. "Came to *me*. Now *I* am in control of *you*. And that's the math."

Someone else is in the room. A big guy stands behind Lario with his arms crossed, dark shades hiding his eyes in the already dusky room. He's watching carefully as the scene unfolds.

"Do you want to just… *die*? Or"—Lario lifts his hands dramatically—"join this illustrious world of vampiredom?"

Lario lowers his face to hers, waiting for an answer. He's wearing a sinister grin, and the poor girl is scared out of her head. Even I'm panicking. I remember once seeing a girl get drunk dry by a vampire in an underground tunnel, and I did nothing about it. This one's still alive, and she's still human.

Lario runs his grimy hands up and down her inner thigh. His fingers find their way to her crotch, and he presses there. She hasn't stopped whimpering.

"I will say this"—he licks his lip—"you will definitely be special to me if you choose to roll with the vamps." He snickers, proud of his hip choice of words.

She shakes her head. "Just let me go home. I won't say anything."

He exhales hard, right into her face. He's exaggerating being disappointed. "You want to take my magic for free?"

She shakes her head. "No, I don't want it."

I can't take this anymore. I become aware of my full surroundings, and I'm definitely not in the Black Hills. I hear hard music in the background. Red lights flow from the main room, which is separated from this room by a short corridor.

Lario drops his head in surrender and looks back at her. "We could've had so much fun." He stands straight. "Kill her," he nonchalantly orders the human. "I have business to attend to."

So Lario uses human henchmen to exact his will

on other humans. He strides out of the room, leaving the girl alone with this big guy. One thing's for sure—the guy doesn't intend to make it quick and fast for the girl. He licks his lips, salivating at the sexy woman like a starving dog at prime rib. She closes her eyes. She's already given up.

I'm torn.

I can't let Lario get away.

I can't let this poor girl die.

So I hit the beast of a man with sleep. He tumbles to the floor as he takes his first step toward her, instantly passed out. When the girl sees him go down, her eyes expand in disbelief. She doesn't know if she's the luckiest person in the world or if she's still in trouble. I put my hands on her temples, and she looks up at me.

"Do you see me?" I ask.

"Yes," she says, barely audible.

"You will be invisible to the eyes of humans and vampires for one hour. Get out of here now."

I don't have to tell her twice. She leaps off the bed, snatches her coat off the floor, and runs out of there as fast as her feet can carry her. In all my life, I've never felt better than I do at this moment. I saved her life, and by the look of things, she's through with Shams. I hope. Humans have short memories. I think it's a biological coping mechanism. Speaking of Shams, I need to see what "business" Lario had to attend to.

I follow his energy down that short corridor and into a packed nightclub. Scantily clad girls and guys in black leather and lace dance in cages, and topless girls in G-string panties gyrate on stage. Patrons socialize and drink in booths or at tables or grind against each other on the dance floor. A number of couples are involved in the actual act of sex in lit and unlit corners of the room. Now I see what the bedrooms are for.

Lario is nowhere in sight, so I follow his energy out the door and into the night.

Just as I thought, he's not in North Dakota. We're in an unmarked building that borders SoHo and Greenwich in Manhattan. This raunchy club is in the basement of an old brownstone, so I have to move up steep, unlit steps to get to the street. This isn't a real nightclub. There are no lines of eager wannabes or burly doorman waiting outside. The music can't even be heard from the sidewalk.

Lario hasn't gone far. I walk a few feet up the sidewalk, turn down another dark stairway, and walk right through a door. I move cautiously into an empty room with floor-to-ceiling mirrored walls.

Lario isn't alone; to my complete and utter shock, the vampire named Tal is with him—the one who bonded herself to Baron. He scratches the back of his neck as if he's thinking his way out of a conundrum.

I move to the right a little so that I can see what they're watching in the mirror. A tall boy with dark features, his build is similar to Baron's, is in a tiny bedroom with two twin beds. There's one tall bookcase with only one shelf devoted to books; the other three hold cute little knickknacks girls like to collect. Two desks are pushed up against the wall on each side of the room. Although I've never lived in one, this has to be a college dorm.

This tall, good-looking guy is conversing with a pretty girl with long blond hair who's wearing a black hat. Tears stream from her eyes, although she doesn't appear to be crying; instead, she's clearly bewildered.

He asks her, "Do you believe me?"

"I don't have a choice." Her shaky voice sounds so sad. "I can't believe stuff like this happens in real life."

"Me neither," he says with a sigh.

"How did this happen to you?"

"Danny took me to The Door for my birthday."

"The Door?" She frowns, trying to figure out what he's referring too.

"It's one of those strip places. I asked you if you minded me going, and remember you said…"

"As long as you don't let a dirty stripper grind on your lap," she whispers, recalling that particular conversation. Then she wipes the tears from her cheek.

"Yeah," he says. "I didn't get a lap dance, and I only had one drink. I think I was drugged or something."

"Score one for me," Lario sings, as proud as ever. "Where are these idiots anyway?"

"I don't know," Tal admits, gawking at the scene playing out in the mirror.

I study Tal closely. She's quite stunning with long dark hair and gripping bedroom eyes. Jealousy wants to weasel its way inside of me, but I refuse to let it. Of all people, I know that beauty runs wide and skin deep.

"No?" Lario gripes, sounding as if he's about to throw a tantrum.

"Look," she snaps, "we see the vampire and human. Nothing else."

"Then get me more. It's a college dorm, for Christ's sake. Get me a banner, school colors, pom-

poms. She looks like a cheerleader; where's the short skirt and tight sweater with the damn school's name on it!"

"You don't see it because it's not there." She shoves her hand at the mirror. "If it was there, then you would see it. And if I could make it happen, then you would see it." Her mouth and jaw are tight; Lario has clearly pissed her off.

"Then make it happen!"

"You're a Sham too. You make it happen!" She lifts her brows. "If you can."

The two of them engage in a stare down of epic proportions. It looks as if they're on the verge of throwing punches. As always, Lario knows exactly when to retreat. I wonder what he's thinking, but for the moment, this is close enough. Getting into his head may be too risky.

"Where's Ze Feldis?" he asks.

"I lost him…"

"You lost him?" he roars, cutting her off.

"Calm your ass down, Exgesis!" she shouts. "Do you think this is easy?"

He doesn't answer that; again, he's choosing not to devour the hand that's feeding him. But that's all I need to know in order to move forward. I don't know who this kid is, but he's a vampire Lario is

132

interested in, and although *he* was unable to see everything, I could.

"Let's get out of here" is the first thing I say when I return to what looks like a carbon copy of Seward's Icebox.

Baron and Viesel Egos watch me expectantly.

"He's not here. Lario's in New York, and I know who he's looking for."

## CHAPTER 7
# THROUGH MIRRORS

After Viesel Egos takes his hand out of his pocket, he nods at Baron and then at me before shooting off. The vampires remain on the lookout as I climb on Baron's back. Using my instincts, I guide him to the forest that's under the protection of the House of Benel without taking the tunnels.

I'm relying on my instincts these days, which is a huge change for me. I used to fight against my nature so that I could appear "normal," more so to myself than to the others around me. However, without thinking about it, I let my instincts lead us right into the forest, where it's daytime. Baron and I stand under the sun, and amazement shapes both of our facial expressions.

"You're not ashes," I finally say.

Baron has his arms lifted and his sleeves pulled back, studying his uncooked arms. Then he touches his cheeks.

The sun is directly overhead, signaling high noon, and the heat and humidity are starting to mellow. It's clear the forest has had a late summer rain, as the dampness fills the air with the sweet, earthy scent of wet leaves, twigs, and soil. I've never been much of a nature girl, but I can't stop smiling. I never thought I'd get to share a moment like this —time in the sun—with Baron.

"Why?" He stares at me for an answer, but I don't have one.

"It's the veil over the House of Benel," replies Lorenzo, who just transformed from a butterfly to a humanoid. "You can walk in the sun here, Ze Feldis."

Baron's lips are pursed tightly together, and his eyes are watery. *My goodness, he's trying not to cry.*

"This is remarkable," he says past his tight throat.

I don't know how to respond. Part of me wants to give him space and let him feel the full joy of the moment. The other part of me thinks a good girl-friend—because that's what I am now, his girlfriend

136

—would hold his hand or give him a hug or something.

I settle on saying, "I can't imagine hiding from the sun for three hundred and seventy-eight years."

Baron clears his throat. "It's hell." He manages to wink at me as he takes my hand.

"Are you ready, or do you want to stay out here a little while longer?"

He puts his mouth near mine. "How about me, you, and that blue dress of yours take a walk in the woods a little later on?" He slyly glances at Lorenzo. "When we're alone."

"Deal." I smirk. I can never keep my heart from fluttering when he gets this close to me.

Lorenzo looks toward the main property, patiently waiting for our moment to end.

---

WE WALK INSIDE THE HOUSE AND HEAD TOWARD THE library. Baron remarks on how nice the place is as we pass rooms I haven't even seen before. As I stand at the library door, ready to say, *Open*, I hear, *Oh, Cl'auta*.

I know that voice. *Oh, Fawn?*

I tell the door to open. She's in front of the

stacks of Lario's books, holding a book. We beam at each other with glistening eyes.

"I thought I'd surprise you," she says.

"Oh my God, you did!"

I rush to her, and she takes my hands. I can feel a surge of pure happiness flow through me.

"Are you better?" I ask.

"A million times better."

I smooth one side of her cheek. "You have color in your skin." I never knew her skin had a rosy undertone that fits her ginger hair and emerald eyes.

"I know. I've literally been the walking dead ever since I gave Lario the leaf. Father explained how I gave him half of my humanity so that he could be human."

My expression drops upon mention of Lario. How do I explain the web of deception he's weaved? How do I tell a woman that the individual she loved, whose life she spared, is a psychotic, sociopathic vampire warlock who more than likely kept her around to get his hands on the Script? I have no idea what his plans were for her after being turned back into a vampire, but I'm certain they would have led to her demise.

Baron walks over. "Fawn, it's good to see you. You look well."

She smiles. "Thank you, Ze Feldis. I heard you helped carry me to safety, so thank you for that too."

"I wish I would've warned you about *all* that Exgesis is capable of."

Fawn shakes her head. "No, Ze Feldis, I knew who Lario was, every part of him."

"Really?" I ask. "You knew he was a lying murderer? Because I just saved a girl's life after he ordered his human henchman to kill her. Did you know he was capable of that sort of terror?"

Fawn touches my shoulder. "Calm down, Cl'auta. I'm only saying that in all the dark, there's a bright dot of light in him too."

"I don't think so," I counter with a snarl. I don't think I ever snarl.

She's alarmed by my reaction. I'm not editing any part of what I'm showing her because I will make sure he's put to an end when the time comes. In my mind, it's not *if* he's going to die; it's *when* he's going to die. And I don't have to worry about Fawn hearing my thoughts. I've figured out how to block them from her. However, Lorenzo is watching me with concern as well, but I still have no regret. I lift my eyebrows defiantly at him.

"Falu," Lorenzo says to fill the awkward silence. "I'm Lorenzo, Wek to the power of mind of the House of Benel."

I realize that I'm still feeling for Fawn's thoughts and emotions when I'm struck by a dizzy feeling, as if I've just been lifted off the ground too quickly. Fawn and Lorenzo stare into each other's eyes for a moment and look away. I'm not sure what I just felt or saw between them, but I wonder if an attraction between them is possible. He's a Wek.

Fawn puts her focus back on me. "So I'm here" —she wiggles her fingers for us—"with my power of force. Where do we go from here?"

Lorenzo leads us to an interesting swimming pool at the back of the house. It has levels of tunnels, waterfalls, and tide pools that seem to go on forever, like our own backyard tropical paradise. I look at it, wondering when we will ever have the time or desire to explore this monstrosity.

None of us pay "Pleasureville" much attention. We take seats in decorative black, wrought-iron chairs situated around a matching table beneath two gigantic canopy-shaped trimmed trees. A spread of berries, cream, and bread is set upon the tabletop. Fawn and I are the only two beings out of the four of us who actually eat. At least, I think we're the only two; I'm not sure if Weks can eat.

"I wonder who sets up all the food and does the cleaning," I say with pinched eyebrows.

"Maybe the elves," Fawn says.

I actually frown harder, considering the truth in that.

"That was a joke, Cl'auta."

She chuckles, and so do I; even Baron does. I have to remember to be on my toes with her. I'm way more serious than she'll ever be.

"I think there are creatures on this property, but we're invisible to them and they're invisible to us. They set the tables and clean up around us," she says.

"You're guessing?"

"Yes—but it's a good guess, don't you think?"

I chuckle. "No, but really? Wouldn't we bump into each other at some point?"

"We won't." She sounds sure about that.

"Why not?"

"I don't know; have you ever?"

Then I think about it. I never saw the cleaners in Bel Air, Cambridge, or Manhattan. "I guess not."

Fawn grins. My seriousness amuses her. I wish I

could keep the mood light, but it's time to get her caught up on her ex-boyfriend.

Baron bathes in a strip of sun on his side of the table, and Lorenzo listens attentively as I fill Fawn in on how Lario is looking for a vampire with the power of the sun. I tell her about Greece and the universe of vampires living in Mount Olympus. Then I tell her about Shams and how Lario's a sorcerer. That surprises her.

*Of all the things that should shock her about Lario, it's that?* Then I tell her about seeing Tal, which Baron hears for the first time too.

He pounds his fist on the table. "What?"

"From what I gather, Lario has a whole host of people doing his dirty work. You know he's got that golden tongue. So yeah, she's performing magic for him, and he's cracking the whip."

I can see that Baron is greatly disturbed by that. However, we have no time to harp on what he might be feeling. Minutes are passing, and Lario is on the hunt.

"He found the vampire who holds the power of the sun," I say. "It's a college kid. The good thing is that Tal could only give Lario a partial picture of this vampire and his human target. But I could see everything."

Lorenzo pulls his brows together. "There's a reason why he couldn't see."

"What do you mean?" I ask.

"The power of the sun must've already been ignited in the vampire."

"Which means he's in contact with the Life Blood," I conclude.

"Yes."

Fawn and I stare at each other with dread.

"That means Lario could get two for one," I say.

"Potentially." Lorenzo sounds so calm.

Fawn and I shoot to our feet at the same time.

*We have to go get her*, she says to me.

*Right now*, I agree.

Since I'm standing, Baron stands too.

"Which sister holds the power of the sun?" I ask Lorenzo.

He rises to his feet as well. "I don't know. The daughters of the House of Benel are hidden until they're found."

"Well, how many of us are still hidden?" I ask.

"Two. Zillael and Glo," Fawn answers.

"So it's either/or."

"Clarity," Baron says to get my attention. "If the vampire has already been in contact with your sister, he's sure as hell going back to her. Follow him."

---

Baron and I hold hands to activate the full power of light, and I recall the face of the vampire with the power of the sun. He's moving up the snow-covered yard of a house, which has protection spread across the sky above it and beyond. Only if he's bonded with the Life Blood can he actually enter the protection. That's why Baron was able to get into my building in Cambridge.

The vampire gets to the front door and leaps on the rooftop. He pries open a sliding glass ceiling and drops down onto a patio. I walk right through the wall of the home and down a hallway, where I see him climb in bed with a girl. She stirs for a moment, and when she realizes she's not alone, she lets out a loud gasp.

"It's just me," he whispers.

She slides off the bed and creeps over to shut the door. Apparently there are parents nearby. I'm reading his mind, and hers too. Something pretty sexual is going to happen between them very soon. They're too attracted to each other; it's the same uncontrollable passion I have for Baron. I've seen enough; they're safe under the protection for now.

When I return to my full self, all eyes are on me.

"They're together," I say.

"Are they safe?" Fawn asks.

"Yes, they are. And they're *together*, together. You know"—I look at Baron—"like you and I are together. He called her Zillael in his mind, and she knows him as Vayle."

"We should go get them," Baron says.

"Yeah, but I think we should do it in the morning."

"Why?"

"Because the sun is supposed to be out when I reach him."

"But I can't go with you if the sun is up."

"I know. But Fawn can."

Baron scratches the back of his neck in frustration. He does that when he's upset.

I take his arm and slide his fingers between mine. "She and I will make a formidable opponent for any vampire. We've done it before."

"That's true, Ze Feldis," Fawn says.

Baron looks me deep in the eyes. "You'll take my light with you?"

"Won't leave home without it." I grin, attempting to make a joke.

It must've worked because Fawn chuckles a little.

Baron is so worried that he totally missed it. "All right." His tone makes it clear he's giving in but not happily. "But we need to know what you're going to be facing."

He suggests I see how far Lario's gotten in his quest to find the vampire named Vayle. Baron and I join hands, and I end up in the mirror room again. Lario's alone, his arms folded across his chest as he watches a scene in one of the mirrors. His body language tells me that he's in control of what's going on in that place.

I take a few cautious steps to stand behind him. I've created a shield of invisibility, but when he flicks his head around and narrows his beady eyes at the doorway, I realize I need to add silence to my veil of protection. I see the same college dorm room. The pretty blond girl from earlier is sitting in bed, flustered from being awakened.

"Who is it?" she calls. She asks again, this time louder.

"Danny," a guy answers.

She narrows her eyes on a clock on a desk

against the wall. "What do you want?" She frowns. He is not a welcomed caller.

"Did you see Vayle?" Danny says as low as possible from behind the door.

As she slips out of bed, wraps a robe around her, and slogs over to the door, I remember that Danny is the name of the person Vayle said took him to a strip joint called The Door. She opens the door, and there stands a suave fellow with high designer jeans, gelled-back auburn hair, and a very expensive watch. He's nervous, although he's trying to hide it, and scared too.

"Yeah, he stopped by. Why?"

He glances down both ends of the hallway. "Can you let me in, Sabrina? I saw him too, and I want to talk to you about it."

"Can we talk tomorrow? I'm tired."

"Did he say he was a vampire?" He asks that quickly as a way to convince her to let him in.

He thinks she'll want to take their bizarre conversation about "vampires" indoors. Sabrina is speechless. She had been hoping her conversation with Vayle in which he convinced her he was a vampire was a terrible nightmare and, up until this very moment, that's what she led herself to believe.

His tactic works, and she steps back to let him in. They sit down on the edge of her bed.

"Where's Cassie?" he asks, speaking of the girl the other bed belongs to.

"She's spending the night with Regan. So… he told you that too, that he's a vampire?"

"Do you believe it?" he asks.

She shrugs. "He doesn't look the same. He's all in shape, and his face looks a little different. Maybe it isn't him?"

"It's him." Danny has no doubts about it.

"Are you sure?" She still doesn't look convinced.

"I'm sure."

"Oh."

"Did he say where he's living?" Danny asks.

"That's it," Lario says encouragingly. He's on the tips of his toes, hanging on their every word.

"No, he didn't." She takes a thoughtful pause. "Wait! He said something about some place in Moonridge."

"Bingo!" Lario sings.

I'm trying to keep my eye on Lario and monitor the scene that's playing out.

"I'm done with her," Lario says dismissively. "Make her choose."

Apparently Danny can hear him. "Yeah,

well…" Danny fidgets through the pockets of his black leather coat.

Sabrina watches him curiously. She's thinking maybe he has a letter or something from Vayle. But I know what he has, and that's when I decide it's time to join them.

Now I'm standing in front of Sabrina and Danny. She has no idea what trauma she'll be facing in a few seconds if I don't intervene. He's searching for a syringe to shoot her up with a drug. Tal is waiting at the front steps of the building to carry Sabrina out. I see all of those plans in Danny's head, so I muddy his thoughts.

"Well, what?" Sabrina is watching him, perplexed.

"Well…" he says.

It worked. He's confused.

"Do you believe it? Do you think he's some kind of vampire?" she asks.

"Who?"

"Vayle?"

"*Vayle*? He's missing, right?"

Now she's worried that maybe Danny's high. She knows he gets wasted more times than not, and she always had a problem with Vayle hanging out with him. She's always suspected Danny had something to do with Vayle's disappearance, maybe even his reappearance.

Danny looks around the room, trying to figure out how in the world he got there. The confusion I'm hitting him with is working, but I'm not done.

*Reach into the inside of your coat pocket and take out the syringe*, I tell him.

He slips it out of his coat pocket and holds it up. Sabrina jumps to her feet. She's on the verge of yelling, so I zap her with indifference.

*Tell me what it is*, I say to Danny.

*Liquid Rohypnol.*

*Date rape drug?*

*Yes.*

I tell him to empty the contents into the trashcan and put the syringe back in his pocket, which he does. I send Sabrina back to sleep while I follow Danny out of the building. He descends the steps to where Tal is waiting for him. Due to my veil of protection around him, he's unable to see or hear her, and she can't get near him.

"Is she ready?" Tal asks.

Danny rushes right past her. She jumps, intending to block his path, but the shield sends her flying far into the night, shrieking in pain. The good thing is it's early in the morning and no one is around.

Tal looks toward Sabrina's building, but I put a shield over it too. Tal turns in circles, snarling at the air.

"I know you're here," she hisses, low and throaty. "The one with the Power of Mind."

I don't say anything.

"How's Ze Feldis?" she sneers at the emptiness. "I bet you think he belongs to you?"

Still, I remain quiet.

She gropes her breasts and her belly and her crotch. "I bet you think he didn't touch me, rub me, and make me scream. He's so good at it, isn't he?"

That's when I've had enough. I create a shield of protection on this campus against all vampires. Not only does Tal screech and race off, but I see other lines of red vapor shoot out from beneath the veil. There were more vampires here. A lot more.

When I come back to myself, I tell Baron, Fawn, and Lorenzo what just happened.

"This is the second girl I had to save from Lario in less than two hours!" I'm breathing heavily and shaking a little, upset by being taunted by Tal. Of course, I don't tell Baron about that. She may have upset me, but I believe in our love. He chose me, not her. However, I do dread that I may have to contend with another Zina in the future.

"So Exgesis found her?" Baron asks.

"He's a monster."

"Don't say that, Cl'auta," Fawn admonishes me in her gentle way.

I don't retort. I could live nine lives and never comprehend the compassion she has for that soulless monster. I tell them that Lario knows Vayle is in Moonridge, Maine. We agree to stick to the plan and not divert from the Script. Fawn and I will bring them here in *their* morning.

## CHAPTER 8
# COLLECTING THE SUN

We have a lot of hours to kill, so I suggest that Baron and I go for that walk in the forest.

"You *can* read my mind," he says with a smirk.

My knees turn to jelly, but I tell him to give me a minute to change shoes. I run into the house and return wearing a pair of flat sandals. We wander out into the woods, walking at normal speed through the trees facing the descending sun. I yawn, which I rarely do, as we weave through Indian trails.

Baron says, "It's been a long day for you."

I glance at him; even shifting my eyes feels like a chore. "Yeah." I force myself to smile at him.

"I don't think you're doing so well. Is everything okay?" he asks.

I shrug. When life turns heavy, I clam up and go inside myself to figure it all out. He wants to drag all of my concerns out of me. I don't mind sharing, but it's strange that another person is trying to make me. He waits for me to say something.

"Lario is a true sociopath," I say. "You should've seen how dismissive he was about taking the lives of those two girls. It was either become a vampire or die."

Baron grunts.

"What?"

"We don't like turning humans into vampires. One more vampire means more competition for blood. The less of us there are, the easier it is to get quenched."

"So he's working against his own interest?"

"I wouldn't say that..." Baron stops short because he's distracted by the sight of a slow-moving stream cutting through a narrow ravine. Streaks of sunlight fill the space between the oak trees that line both sides of the stream and dance on the water's surface.

"I know; it's lovely." I wrap my arms around Baron's waist from behind. When he switches positions, I get the effect I was seeking—feeling safe and consumed by his strength.

"I was saying," he continues with his lips against my ear, "you're right to be wary of Exgesis. Everything he's ever done has been self-serving. But his weakness is his self-preservation. If everyone else falls, he wants to be the last one standing."

"So right now he's using Tal to do his dirty work?" I close my eyes and sigh.

Baron faces me. "Clarity, did we make this walk to discuss Tal?" He nibbles on my top lip.

"No," I whisper, defenseless against his sensual powers.

"So…" He smirks. "We have a sun. We have water. We have grass. I have your body. What do you want to do with it all?"

He's right of course; he always is. It's time to relieve the tension of the long hours already spent. It's time to let down my guard and be who Baron inspires me to be.

"Last one there is a rotten egg," I say.

He beams at me. "Where?"

I twist around to point to the sparkling stream. "There."

As he looks at it, I try to take off, but he has me around the waist. I've never laughed this hard, twisting to get loose. It's so childish! I call him a cheater, and then he reminds me who tried to cheat first. He finally lets me go and zooms past me like a flash of light. Before I can complete three good strides, he's in the stream in briefs and a white tee shirt.

"Who runs and gets naked at the same time? You should take that act to the circus." I laugh.

We kick water at each other and follow the creek toward a shallow lake, where we splash around. We lie out on a grassy mound to dry off. Baron peels my dress open. He uses a divine compilation of his teeth, tongue, and lips to taste my neck, my breasts, down to my waist. I'm caught in a state of euphoria when he spreads my legs, brings my nether regions close to his mouth, and circles his tongue around my clit. He stays right there, making me moan, pant. He's merciless. My fingers rake the grass. The sounds he makes tell me he enjoys the way I taste. I must admit, that's such a turn-on. I twist, wanting to escape his tongue and wanting more of it. The ticking sensation ignites deep in my groin, and I scream.

"You taste so good," Baron whispers. He growls and pushes his pulsing erection inside of me, stroking me as if it's the first time he's ever taken me.

I almost forget about Lario, the young vampire named Vayle, and the seventh sister. Baron rolls me on top of him and squeezes my butt as he thrusts me against his erection. His mouth covers my nipple, and I'm on the verge of climaxing when Lorenzo says, *Cl'auta. It's time.*

---

LORENZO ASSURES BARON THAT HE'S BEEN FULLY accommodated at the House of Benel. I show Baron to my quarters, and in the bedroom is a wardrobe of men's clothing. I'm pretty sure those garments weren't there before.

Baron shuffles through the clothes, touching them and smelling them. "These are mine." He sounds surprised.

I still have a blithe feeling in my heart, so I take a whiff of one of his crisp white shirts. I moan. "Smells like Baron Ze Feldis."

He gives me those eyes, but we both know there's no time to indulge.

Lorenzo shows Baron to an office where he can conduct business while I prepare to recover the vampire with the power of sun. I take a quick shower and put on a pair of black pants and a black shirt. Once I'm dressed, I stare at myself in the mirror. It's been a long time since I've taken a long look at Clarity Parker. Physically, nothing has changed. I still have too much hair. I have the same heart-shaped face, bright brown eyes, and pouty lips. It's still pretty eerie how Fawn, Adore, and I look exactly alike.

When I'm ready, I meet Fawn, Baron, and Lorenzo in the library. I've never carried Baron's light in my physical self, but we give it a try. After holding hands and connecting, I visualize myself gathering his light and filling myself with it. When I release his hands, I can still feel him swirling inside of me, so it must've worked. I focus on the vampire Vayle until his energy tugs at me and guides me to him.

"Let's go get him," I say to Fawn.

"After you, Captain," she replies.

We smile at each other. It seems like forever since we've hit the road together. I love Baron, but I also love that my sister and I are doing this alone. It makes it seem less severe, although I know it isn't. But I know she won't pull out silver daggers or a blazing sword and chop off someone's head or burn them to ashes.

Fawn and I ride the wind to Moonridge. I've put a shield of blindness over us because we're moving over populated areas. She's very silent. I know we have to have a conversation about Lario. I *need* to know how and where she met him. I *want* to know how in the dickens she could ever fall in love with him. I also *want* to know how I could be around him for a few days and perceive that something wasn't quite right about him, yet she could live with him for years and not get it.

I peek at her. She's looking straight ahead. Although her expression is blank, I can see her mind isn't. I choose not to enter it. I want to hear her speak the answers to my questions.

"Is the Selell still under protection?" she asks.

"He is. He's in what looks like a living room, and others are around him. And…" I see that the curtains are pulled from the windows, the morning light flooding into the room. "He isn't burning from the sunlight."

"Could that be the power of the sun? He can go out in the daytime," she asks as we hit fog.

It's colder than the already icy east coast winter air, and it's so dense I can barely see her beside me.

"They're here," she whispers. She aims her hand forward to unleash a force that blows the fog away. Her wind is so powerful it clears out the snow clouds too.

I keep monitoring what's going on in the living room. I've been so focused on the vampire that I forgot about Zillael. Right now, a petite blond woman is studying a mark on the back of Zillael's shoulder and then the vampire's shoulder, comparing the two. They're two half-suns that make a whole. I gasp.

"What?" Fawn asks.

I tell her about the birthmarks. "It's the same symbol in the Script."

"This is all becoming real," she marvels.

I'm relieved she's just as shocked by it all as I am. "I know." I sigh.

That's when I see Zillael rushing out the house, chasing the beautiful boy who was in the room, the one with light brown hair, green eyes, and delicate facial features. My money's on him being a Wek.

Alarmed, I grab Fawn's arm. "She ran out of the protection."

Fawn's eyes grow. She raises both hands to double the force of her power as we increase our pace. I'm moving so fast the ground becomes a blur.

I do wish I had Baron's speed right now. I wish he could transfer *that* over to me. My heart knocks against my chest so hard I feel the vibrations in my throat. I see the two of them rolling around in the snow.

"What the heck?!" I shout. "She's in the woods, making out with one of the guys. He's a Wek, I think."

Now we're both frowning hard.

"Wait. The fog has rolled in over them, so he stopped. They're out of the woods." I call it as quickly as I see it.

"Are we almost there?" she shouts.

"Almost. They're all standing in a defensive circle, ready to fight, but your force is blowing right past them."

I see out into the woods where beings that were once vampires convulse and cry out in agony. Hundreds of them are all shriveling up at the same time, but I also see mounds of ashes that have been there before Fawn's force cleared the fog. And then I see the culprit: a man in all black with glowing blue eyes like those of Viesel Egos. He's clutching a sword of fire, and once there is no more fog, he simply disappears.

When our feet touch the ground, the group of

five watches us curiously. It's obvious which one is Zillael. Like her sisters, she stands out. Her long spiraling hair is black, and her eyes are an odd yellow. Her skin has the same complexion as a ripening peach. Her mouth, nose, and eyes are sharp against her delicate heart-shaped face.

"And another one found," Fawn whispers.

"What was once hidden," I whisper back.

---

IT'S NIGHTTIME AT OUR ESTATE. ZILLAEL AND VAYLE examine the dark forest with wide eyes. I explain the time difference the best way I know how. I say something about the continuum and the merging of Earth and Enu, adding that maybe diamonds and a protective shield created by our father have something to do with it. However, both continue to study me with confusion.

We all easily lift ourselves over the gate of trees. I see that Zillael is already aware of her speed and natural buoyancy. Even riding the wind wasn't a foreign concept to her. As soon as we're on the other side of the gate, I stand face to face with Baron, who draws me into him.

"You made it."

Zillael has the same reaction that all females have at first. Her mouth falls open and her eyes bulge, appreciating the makings of Baron Ze Feldis.

After he sees that I'm not hurt in any way, Baron focuses on the group of newcomers. "You must be Zillael." He extends his hand.

"Wow," she replies, unable to look away. Her eyes naturally fall downward to his physique.

Fawn and I snicker.

*That's the power of Ze Feldis*, Fawn says only to us.

Zillael smashes her hands over her ears. "Wow, I heard that."

All three of us smile at each other.

"The private conversation," Baron says, rewarding us with his delicious smirk.

*Oh my God*, Zillael says. *What in the world is he?*

*He's an anomaly*. Fawn laughs.

"So are you two married or something?" Vayle, the vampire asks, waving a finger between Baron and me.

"No," I say defensively, which makes Baron turn to me with a frown. "But we're together."

"Damn. You two must have awesome sex."

I'm shocked. I wish I could've anticipated him saying that and somehow stopped the words from coming out of his mouth.

"Zillael, why don't you go get dry and meet us up there." Fawn points to the balcony on the second level.

"I'll show you to your space," Derek, Zill's Wek, says. He glances at Vayle. "And you too."

They're clearly not friends.

"Wait, shouldn't I sleep with the Power of the Sun?" Vayle asks, trying to get under Derek's skin. "Our birthmarks prove that we're two halves of a whole."

"No," Derek grunts before Fawn or I can answer.

"But don't you two sleep together?" Vayle shifts a finger between Baron and me again. Apparently the kid has no filter.

"Hey," Baron reproves him as I say, using the same tone of voice, "I'm not seventeen."

Zillael elbows him. "Vayle, stop. Please."

He shrugs as they take off. "I'm just saying, that's all."

"Well, stop it. Don't say anything because you're embarrassing me."

"You and I are hot like those two. We're going to have awesome sex too!"

"You're an idiot."

They go back and forth until they're out of

sight, neither wanting to give the other the last word.

When the rest of us arrive on the balcony, the invisible servants have already set the table with berries, cream, bread, and Goshem tea. Vayle arrives at the table before Zillael and her Wek.

"I saw you yesterday in the dorm room," I reveal to him, ready to get the first round of questioning over.

"You did?" He sounds doubtful.

"You were with Sabrina, and you told her you were a vampire."

"You know Sabrina?"

"No, I don't. But Danny stopped by later that night."

"Danny?"

"Danny," I say. "You told Sabrina that Danny took you to a place called The Door?"

"Yeah." He still sounds surprised.

"This Danny's been getting friendly with vampires. Did you know that?"

Vayle shakes his head. "No."

"Is he a drug dealer?"

"I mean, there are rumors, but I never saw him sell anything."

I nod as I open up to read his thoughts. I don't

believe him. He's cursing himself for trusting Danny, using dirty words that are not in my vocabulary.

"Listen," I begin, "when he came to her room, he was going to drug her with the date rape drug. A vampire named"—I glance at Baron, who's been sitting beside me, listening silently—"Tal was waiting to take her somewhere."

"Did they take her?" Vayle asks as he scoots to the edge of his seat. That information was enough to turn off his cool and flippant disposition.

I shake my head. "No, I stopped him. But he's in cahoots with some pretty evil vampires." I glance at Fawn after I say that, and her expression doesn't change. She's still interested in what I'm saying, waiting to add to the conversation if need be. I'm relieved. "These vampires are very interested in your power of the sun. I'm just wondering if that's the reason you were turned."

"He's like me," Baron chimes in.

"What do you mean?" Vayle asks.

"I guess we can call vampires like us 'first generation,' and the ones who come from Exgesis 'second generation.'"

"The ones who can drink other vampires," I conclude.

"Wait," Vayle exclaims. "That night… the night I ran into Zill, I was attacked by three vampires!"

"Were they trying to drink you?" Baron asks.

"Dry!" He rubs the side of his neck. "I couldn't believe it."

Baron and I give each other looks.

"Lario didn't know," he says.

"It doesn't seem like it," I say. "It just so happened to be. Like fate or something."

All of us stare at Vayle, whose frown shows how conflicted he is. I get in his mind. He's remembering the thirst before he met Zillael and the days of being doomed to the darkness. He's questioning whether fate has been kind to him for putting him through that kind of hell.

Baron studies me as I read Vayle's mind. I decide to leave those thoughts to Vayle, though. Fate will just have to convince the young vampire whether it has been kind to him.

About an hour passes before Zillael and the Wek appear. Her eyes are a little red, like she's been crying. There's definitely tension between her and Derek as she takes her seat beside Fawn. He sits at the opposite end of the table beside Lorenzo.

I notice Zillael's wearing a pair of overalls that are two sizes too big and a faded gray oversized T-shirt. I'm wondering if she actually pulled that messy ensemble out of her closet. Surely Felix wouldn't let such an outfit enter the house. It's clear she's hiding her beauty, and I wonder why. Fawn, being the gentle creature she is, takes Zillael's hand and rubs the back of it. Zillael looks down and then into Fawn's eyes, confused.

"I think it's time we explain as much as we can to our sister, Falu," I say.

Zillael watches us with expectant, glassy eyes. She's quite pained by whatever happened between her and Derek. Plus, she's still affected by the disappearing act her guardian, Deanna, pulled. She's known Deanna as her mother from the day she was born. While Zillael was caught up in the amazement of seeing Fawn and me for the first time, her guardian disappeared into thin air. When she finally realized that Deanna was gone, Zillael wanted to run back home to see if she could find her there. Derek, her Wek, assured her that Deanna was not at the house.

"One day you might see her again," he'd said to soothe her agony.

"What do you mean by *might*?" Zillael had bitterly asked. "Are you saying that's it?"

He'd taken her shoulders and stared deeply into

her eyes. "It's time to take the next step, Zill. Her job was to keep you hidden. You're not hidden anymore."

Her eyes had skipped from me to Fawn to Vayle, and then she simply whispered, "Okay."

She had followed us, carrying her sadness with her. At that moment, I knew she was definitely my sister—no tantrums, no whining or crying. She just gutted it up and carried on. She's a girl raised by a true *guardian*.

Right now, we're at the table, and Fawn is telling her the story of Zillael, the grandmother she's named after, and the conversation she had with the angel at the waterfalls.

"Wow! She just asked for her village to be spared and she got us," Zillael sums it up. "Doesn't seem fair."

Fawn shakes her head. "No, she was happy to sacrifice. She didn't know the depths of her heart, but the Creator did. I look at it this way: if Zillael had faced a vampire, she would've asked that it be restored."

Unexpectedly, Vayle says, "It makes sense to me."

I read his thoughts and emotions. This is the

best news he's heard since last year, since the day he was turned into a Selell.

As Fawn talks about Enu, I excuse myself to go consult the Script. For some strange reason, I feel it calling me. Baron and Lorenzo accompany me.

---

I'M IN THE DIAMOND CHAMBER GETTING READY TO read the Script. But before doing so, I look out at Baron and Lorenzo having a discussion by the bookcase. Then they scan the spines of shelved books. After my curiosity passes, I look down at the scroll and read.

*The light finds might—the sun is won. The force of the sun and sun with sun for the light opens Box of Jari.*

Then there's the head of a daughter, whom I identify by the wavy hair. She's lifting a stone and facing half the sun. Next I see the full sun, the symbol of the house of Benel, and the symbol that represents me, holding the key. What must be the Box of Jari is represented by a three-dimensional block. Then there's a peculiar map that contains only arrows and representations of landmarks—a tree, mountains, and depressions in the ground.

I'm studying it, attempting to remember every

detail, when a blast of light fills the chamber. I'm blinded. A brighter ray of light hits me, and I feel the warm beam pour up my nose and down my throat. All of my limbs are buoyant. If I wanted to blast off to the moon, I'm sure I could get there faster than a speeding rocket. And then in a flash, it's all gone. Baron and Lorenzo are still combing through books. I'm sure they didn't see what just happened.

Every single detail of the map is etched in my memory. I step out of the diamond encasement; Baron and Lorenzo watch me expectantly.

"Anything new?" Baron asks, eager for information.

"I have a map that leads to the Box of Jari." I turn to Lorenzo to see if he shows signs of recognition.

"Never heard of it," he says, reading the question in my expression.

"The map is in my head, and we must travel by riding the wind. Also, we're supposed to move only during the day and be protected by the Power of the Sun."

"Wait"—Baron lifts his hands—"I can be in the sun here, but not out there."

"I know," I whisper, shaking my head. But the

combined power of light is needed. Together, Baron and I form Adore's power as long as she's not on Earth. Not only is it an influencer, it's one of our weapons. "But we do have the power of the sun."

Baron and Lorenzo watch me; I see their thoughts turning.

---

IT's EARLY AFTERNOON BEYOND THE BORDERS OF our property. But in here, we're walking through the dark, peaceful forest. The summer clouds have cleared. The stars twinkle above us, and the moonlight glistens across the treetops. The only sound comes from the twigs crunching beneath our feet.

We've already discussed it; Vayle will step out into the sun first, along with Fawn. Next, Baron will enter Earth's real time. If he starts to burn, Fawn will blow him back into the woods. Baron has assured me that, if he begins to burn, he will heal in a few days. We all stop at the border between the protected forest and the unprotected forest, where the snow has fallen between the trees.

"I guess I'm up first," Vayle says. He looks between Baron, Lorenzo, and me for validation.

"You are," I confirm.

Vayle steps out into the daylight. Fawn follows him. I take Baron's hand. In that moment, I want to renege, maybe find another way. But Vayle isn't burned. It's Baron's turn.

He has to pry my hand out of his. "Don't worry, Clarity. I'll live no matter what." He grins, attempting to calm my nerves.

I nod stiffly. "I know." I force a weak smile. The truth is, *I hope*.

He steps over the border until he's fully covered in the daylight. We're all watching him, waiting for his skin to catch fire. It doesn't. I step out into the daytime with Zillael, who's smiling at Vayle.

Lorenzo searches over each shoulder and tilts his head back to glare at the sky. "We should get back into the protection now."

He doesn't have to tell any of us twice. We shuffle back in to the forest and just in time. We look into the daylight and see dark shadows swooping over the trees we just left.

"It senses the vampires," Lorenzo explains.

"Vampires? Why?" Vayle's panicked.

"It just does. It's nothing to worry about," Derek assures him.

"What's *it* anyway?"

"It's the reason why you exist, and it's what we're fighting."

Derek and Vayle give each other a final look before ending the discussion. Vayle is realizing that Derek is not only Zillael's Wek, but his too. As we walk back, I tune into everyone's thoughts. Vayle's hoping that his display has finally convinced Zillael that she belongs with him and not Derek.

I tap into Zillael and Derek's thoughts to learn what happened between them. This afternoon, Derek told her he was falling for her, but he couldn't bond with her if he's to be her Wek. He vowed to keep his distance for the greater good. As Fawn told Zillael everything about Enu, our grandmother, and our father, it began to sink in. But not until Zillael saw Baron stand in the daylight and took in all of our reactions did the responsibility of being a Life Blood creature finally sink in. Zillael glances at Vayle. Her pulse shoots up because of the way he looks at her. It's the way vampires gaze at you when they want to ravish your body. I know that look all too well, and it is so very hard to resist.

Fawn... Well, her thoughts are blank, and I think that's on purpose.

After we all lift ourselves over the gate and start

up the lawn, I kiss Baron on the cheek. "I'll see you in bed."

"Where are you going?" he asks, almost as if he isn't happy about my possible delay.

"I need to talk." My eyes dart over to Fawn.

Baron nods. He looks at the group. "See you all at Earth's sunrise."

"I'll be here to have your back, bro," Vayle teases.

Baron chuckles a little before taking off. I think Vayle may be growing on him, and that's always good, especially considering the voyage that's ahead of us.

"So tomorrow it's all happening, right?" Zillael asks with dread in her voice.

"Yes," I say as gently as I can, knowing exactly what we're about to face—what *she's* about to face. I wrap my arm around her waist, and she rests her head on my shoulder. "But you're equipped to handle whatever's thrown at us. You're our might, our warrior."

Vayle steps up to her other side. "So you'll be kicking some ass, like you did that night. Remember what you did to those vampires?"

"One of them," she answers and peeks at Derek, who's refusing to look at her.

I see in her mind that he actually took care of two more second-generation vampires.

"You were on your way to putting their lights out though," Vayle says, both to encourage her and to keep Derek out of the equation.

She smiles weakly at no one in particular. Just like the Wek, her heart aches. It's so funny how this happens. It happened with Fawn and Adore and now with Zillael too. It feels as if we grew up together, as if we've been sisters in love all of our lives. I kiss her gently on the forehead.

"Get rest," I say out loud. *And this time you should keep Mr. Octopus Hands out of your bed,* I say only to her.

Her eyes widen. *You saw that?*

*Not all of it, but enough.*

*I don't know how to say no to him,* she confesses.

I understand the intense sexual desire toward vampires. Their ability to stimulate arousal is an unfair advantage.

*Do you love him?* I ask.

*No, I don't think so.*

*Then that's how you say no to him.*

She sighs, frustrated because that's easy to say but a weak motivation to make him keep his hands off of her. *Yeah*. She leans her head forward and looks at Fawn beside me. *Night, Falu*.

*Night, Zillael*, Fawn replies.

"Night, all," Zillael says out loud.

Before Derek or Vayle could respond, she shoots off. Both guys look at each other to see who's going to follow.

"Not sleepy, going for a swim," Vayle announces and shoots off toward the back of the property. He wants to explore the enormous swimming pool.

Once Vayle is gone, Derek nods at the three of us before disappearing.

Fawn and Lorenzo glance at each other awkwardly before she sings, "Night, Lorenzo."

He nods, keeping his gorgeous black eyes glued to her face for a few seconds, then he nods at me. He transforms into a butterfly and flutters away.

Fawn and I head to her space in the house. Instead of being built up, hers fans out into one large open-air room that covers the span of the house. It's very garden-like with flower-patterned furniture and fixtures. She even has a lovely rose garden with a diamond statue of a woman carrying a pot on her shoulder.

"Caviar and crêpes," I say, looking around as I kick off my shoes and sit on a hefty chaise longue.

She chuckles a little. "Yes, this is my taste; Veil Green was all Lario."

"Yes, Lario." I sigh. "He's terrorizing the human world these days."

Fawn perches on the sofa across from me. She sets her chin on her knees for moment to think. "I saw him for the first time at the Linda Morris Suffrage Rally in Washington, DC. It was 1917, and I was a member of the National Women's Party."

"Wow," I say. "What an extraordinary movement to be part of."

"Yes, that's one of the privileges of being alive for such a long time. You can choose to help make history when you want to. Or you can skip it all together."

"I never took you for being the politically active type."

"I know." She closes her eyes to sigh with dread. "I lost myself after I met Lario."

I shake my head. "No, Falu. Lario found a way to steal you from yourself."

Silence lingers between us.

"After you found me in the basement and I woke up in Enu, it felt like I'd been asleep forever. I was searching myself, trying to find this *love* I had for him but…"

"You didn't love him."

"Not in the way you love Ze Feldis. I love Lario's soul though."

"But he's soulless."

"Don't say that," she corrects me.

"I understand why you can't see that." I scratch the back of my neck out of frustration, like Baron does. Once I realize I picked up his habit, I drop my hand. "I've read the hearts of men for thirty years. I've run across people like him. So… narcissistic and self-gratifying that every soul outside of his is simply a paper doll to him. It's dangerous when the mind and heart view the flesh of others as a textile. You see, it's easy to light a match to it."

"I have hope in him, Cl'auta. You should too. Didn't you hear what the Wek said? We're fighting the evil—not its victims."

I don't respond because, between our two view-points, I know I'm in the wrong. Where she has hope, I have hate. At this moment, that hate isn't even close to changing. But it's time to ask the question that's been nagging me ever since this mission began.

"If I'm forced to kill him, will you hate me?"

## CHAPTER 9
# ZILL'S TIMES PAST
ZILL

I lie on top of the bed, staring at the ceiling. I remember the moments before the fog and the wind, which led to the appearance of my two sisters. This still seems insane—*I have sisters. Six of them!*

Fawn and Clarity are so perfect. They know my father. I have a father. *I actually have a father.* Also, I've finally escaped Moonridge, Maine. I'm no longer in high school. I never have to see Riley Simms or Mrs. Lowenstein ever again. I clutch my fists, squeeze my eyes closed, and knock my heels against the mattress in celebration. Unlike Dorothy, I haven't been transported back to that dreary town. Nope. This is home!

I'm free!

When I open my eyes, a face obstructs my view of the ceiling. "Vayle!" I gasp, a little startled. I didn't hear him enter.

Before I know it, he's lying beside me, wearing just pajama bottoms.

"What were you smiling about?" he asks.

I shake my head. "Nothing."

He turns silent. "Hey, shouldn't we generate some power tonight? I have a big role to play tomorrow." He looks at me with that naughty sneer of his.

I scoot away from him. "Don't you have a room?"

He scoots closer to me. "Believe it or not, I do. But it's too far from yours. I think that Wek you *love* is trying to separate us."

"Wait." I sit straight up. "You heard me tell him that?"

Earlier, when Derek had guided me to this unbelievable room, after I had taken in the New-England-cottage-style décor, we happened into an unfortunate discussion.

It began with me saying, "I love you."

Derek had stared at me with the blankest expression. My heart sank, and embarrassment burned my skin. He was showing me that he had no response to that.

"I'm sorry." I'd dropped my face in shame.

"I need to be your Wek," he'd said.

I had lifted my face again. I was kind of mad at Derek. Didn't he just roll around in the snow with me earlier? I would've given myself fully to him if everything that occurred hadn't. "You can't love me and be my Wek too?"

He'd smothered a hard sigh. "You should change." He stepped back from me.

"Maybe I should."

He'd paused. He got the underlying meaning, but I wanted to take it back just as fast as I said it.

"I'll see you shortly, Zill." He'd sounded so unaffected by my ambiguous threat to turn to Vayle. And then he turned around and walked away.

That was earlier, before Vayle and I took an afternoon swim in the pool. We swam underwater the entire time, exploring crystal caves that dropped deeper and deeper into the earth. Not needing to breathe was another miraculous, peculiar thing I'd learned about myself today. That was before Clarity, the more serious of my two sisters, called us out of the water to test a theory. The skin between her eyes remained puckered as she explained the possibilities of the power of the sun and why we'll need it for our journey that starts tomorrow at sun-up.

I think I hid the fact that I was shaking in my boots. I still am. Maybe that's why, although I'd like to take Clarity's advice and follow love instead of lust, the sight of Vayle is a welcomed one.

"I hear everything you say because I'm the one who's bonded to you," Vayle says, bringing me back into the moment.

He stares at me with his hypnotizing, seductive eyes. My broken heart thumps again. Despite the fact that Derek rejected me, I feel like a fraud, a liar who doesn't know what it means to feel authentic love.

"Listen, Zill." Vayle's lying on his side. His hand slides under my T-shirt so that his fingers can do their favorite thing.

I skip a breath as he stimulates one of my nipples. "What are you doing?"

"You're mine now and, who knows, maybe forever. We have fun together, don't we?"

His warm tongue tastes the part of my breast his finger just stiffened. I swallow hard. I can't speak, only moan. He guides his lips onto mine, and we kiss.

This is non-ceasing. The night is evolving. Second by second, he does so many pleasurable things to me, using all those parts of himself that I wish Derek would use. The picture of Derek is fuzzy in my head. I promise myself this is the end, but I cry out after his fingers find their way under my panties, where he uses one of them to massage that sensitive spot. My love for Derek may be already fading; at least, that's what I'm hoping.

## CHAPTER 10

# TAKE TO THE ROAD

I 'm lying in bed on my side, facing Baron, who's facing me. We're in the middle of a long thoughtful pause.

"What did she say?" he asks me.

I stare into his blue eyes. I can see them clearly, even though the lights are out. We decided to keep the curtains open so that he could wake up to sunlight for the first time in over three hundred years.

I sigh. "She said she could never hate me."

"You're not happy with that answer?"

"Yeah, I am, but…" I can barely say.

"Then what's bothering you?"

I whisper, "She said I can't kill Lario because

he's already killing me. And that like her, I should mourn his loss."

Baron smoothes my cheek. "You're the one who's right in this situation."

"Am I?"

He moves me on top of him. His warm mouth gently presses into mine. "You are."

I rest the side of my face on his hard, bare chest. Our energy swirls within me. It's like being wrapped in a soft, warm blanket on a freezing cold night or resting on grass on a perfect sunny day, and doing both with the only man in the entire world I could love. I kiss Baron's chest and close my eyes. Baron's hand slides up and down my back. Instead of giving in to his lust, I give in to his warmth.

Suddenly I'm pulled through blinding light. This doesn't feel like a dream, but I think it's one. I tell myself to wake up, but the insane part is I *am* awake. I look down at myself. The blue tank dress I wear at night is on me. No one ever wears their nightclothes in their dreams. I'm wondering if I should fight back when my body breaks through the wall of light. I see the valley of silver-leafed trees and the translucent mountain range, which I now know is made of diamond.

I'm headed toward one of the many mountain

peaks. The probability of me smashing into it is high. I close my eyes tightly, bracing myself for impact. But I feel nothing as my body flows through the solid compound. I end up standing on my own two feet.

I'm caught in the euphoria of awe. Translucent pillars of purple, green, yellow, and magenta blocks are stacked all around me. A seed of light reflects at the core of each wedge, setting them aglow. The floor is clear too.

"Cl'auta," a familiar voice calls from behind me.

When I flick my face around to see, I feel a presence on the right side of me instead. I turn that way. "Felix? Am I in Enu?"

"Not the human part of you."

Maybe that's why I feel so light on my feet and clear-headed. The lack of sleep from making love to Baron and chasing Lario has worn on me, but now I'm not even mildly exhausted.

"You're about to set foot on a dangerous road," he says.

I just stare at my father. Ever since I was a child, he's garnered this response from me. Part of me wonders if he is a dream. Another part wonders if he'll vanish into thin air. Another part of me asks,

*Who is this man?* It always felt as though I never knew him, and apparently I didn't.

"How is this even happening?" I ask.

"The part of you that's human is still on Earth. The other parts of you are here. But the minutes are passing," he says in a rush. Felix flips up his palm, and right in the middle of it sits the leaf from the Tree of Life, the one I snatched out of Lario's heart. "Keep it with you. When the time comes, you'll know what to do with it."

"I will?" I don't sound too sure of myself.

Then Felix does something that shocks the heck out of me. He takes me by the back of the neck and kisses me on the forehead. *A fatherly gesture.* This has never happened before, ever.

"You will."

I swallow hard. There's no blinking back the tears streaming out of my eyes. I wish they would stop falling. I feel as if they're betraying me. I don't want him to see the hurt child inside of me, the one who wished he'd kiss her on the forehead once— only once—years ago. He presses a finger to my cheek to catch the tears. I'm shocked to see my tears turn into five tiny diamonds in his hands.

"Humph," he grunts, "tears of joy."

The picture of Felix smiling at the diamonds in

his hand is the last thing I see before the light fills my head. I'm moving a thousand miles per hour. My eyes open, and I gasp.

"Clarity?"

Baron's concerned face is the first thing I see. The sunlight floods through the windows, and I'm still lying on top of him.

"Did you have a dream?"

"No," I whisper. There's something in my hand. I look down at the leaf.

Baron scrunches his chin downward to get a better look at it. "What's that?"

"It's the leaf I took from Lario. My father just gave it to me."

"Your father was here?" Baron looks around the room.

"No, I went to him while I was asleep."

"You were here all night. Believe me, I know. It took everything in me not to wake you up."

I snort, amused by that. "The Enuian—I guess I'll call them the 'divine'—sides of me left. You were only groping the human me." I smirk at him.

He chuckles but only briefly. After all, I'm holding a leaf from the Tree of Life.

"What does your father want you to do with it?" He scrutinizes the leaf, not daring to touch it.

"He says I'll know when the time comes." I frown hard.

Baron slides a finger across my crinkled brow. "Relax. You *will* figure things out."

I sigh softly, gazing into his eyes. "I will?"

He kisses me tenderly. "Yes, you will. And you know"—he smirks at me—"we're not going to be alone like this for who knows how long, so… we should take advantage of the time left."

I can *feel* what he wants from me. "Okay. But you have to be still." I stretch across the bed to set the leaf on the nightstand.

"I'm trying, but you can't do what you just did if you want me to be still."

*Goodness, that smirk of his—I'll never be able to resist it.* I take my dress hem and lift it slowly, teasing him.

"Oh man." He closes his eyes to bear the lust.

I must admit this is fun. Baron has always taken control of our lovemaking, unable to contain himself. I chalked it up to him being so intense. I wonder if he was this way three hundred seventy-eight years ago, when he was a human.

He caresses my breasts as soon as I spread my legs and hover above him. "What have you done to me, Clarity?" he whispers thickly.

That's when I pull the hem of my dress up to

my hips. I pull down the top of his pajama pants, shift the crotch of my panties over, and put him inside of me. I slowly shift my hips back and forth, studying his beautiful face. In an instant, he's on top of me, and we're giving it everything we've got. Making love like it's both the first and the last time.

"Damn, I love you," he whispers over and over.

"What do you love about me?" I whisper back.

He nibbles on my neck, making his way to my mouth. "You're smart."

"What else?"

"Resilient."

"What else?"

"Sensitive, passionate, and sexy."

His lips and tongue move down my abdomen.

"Funny," I say, twisting by body, trying to bear the tickle of true pleasure. I'm certain he's discovered every sensitive spot on me and has become an expert at pushing those buttons. "That's everything I love about you."

"That's because we're twin souls."

Hearing him say that makes me snicker. "I didn't know you believed in stuff like that."

When he looks at me with a smirk, his face is right at the major hot spot. "I don't."

I'm only able to chuckle for one second before I end up squirming and moaning in pure pleasure.

The road before us is long indeed. Because Lorenzo the Wek was absolutely right—this part of our relationship is as vital to us as breathing. Going five hours, one day, or even longer than that without indulging in each other will indeed be torture.

---

By noon, I convince Baron that we must stop. I need to feed the human part of me before hitting the road. The sun will rise beyond our sphere at 3:56 p.m. So we take a shower together, making love one more time before departure. While Baron treks off to the house office to make arrangements to keep business running in his absence, I head to the patio dining area where Fawn and Zillael are already eating.

"Coming up for air?" Fawn jokes, fluttering her eyelashes at me.

I roll my eyes a little while grinning so hard my cheeks ache. It appears Zillael has a question for me but is hesitant to ask. But I don't push her, and I stay out of her head.

"I saw, um, Dad." I feel strange calling Felix

that out loud, but he is our father. It's time to get used to calling him that.

"Was he here?" Fawn asks.

Zillael's eyes expand. The very possibility makes her nervous.

"No," I say to put her at ease. "I actually traveled out of myself and to Enu."

"The land that we're sort of from?" Zillael asks.

I nod. "Yeah.

"Why were you there?" Fawn asks.

"He gave me the leaf from the Tree of Life and told me I'll know what to do with it when the time comes."

"You mean the leaf you took from Lario?"

Zillael's eyes move between us, trying to keep up with what we're talking about.

"Yes." I turn to Zillael. "I know Falu explained how we're connected to the Tree of Life."

Her eyes flash to Fawn. "She told me everything."

Fawn smiles at her, which makes Zillael sort of simper bashfully.

"Well, I took a leaf off the Tree of Life and fed it to a vampire," Fawn explains.

"*The* Tree of Life?" Zillael asks.

"We have access to it—but I recommend we steer clear of it."

I lift my hand. "I concur."

"Point taken," Zillael says.

"So," I say with a sigh, "I have the leaf, and at some point, I'm going to have to do something with it."

"What does our father look like?" Zillael asks.

I pause to conjure up a mental picture of him. "Like one of those handsome Egyptian kings you see as relics in a museum exhibit." I hope I can convey how exquisite he is.

"Is he tall? I'm tall. We're all tall," she says.

"He's tall," I confirm.

"And our mother must be beautiful?"

Fawn and I look at each other.

"I've never seen her," I admit.

"But why not?"

"Because it's not time yet," Fawn replies.

"When will the time come?"

Again, Fawn and I consult each other. Fawn nods, giving me the floor.

"We're making it happen right now," I say. "Our father, Felix, has assured me that we have a dangerous road ahead of us. I don't know how long that road is, but maybe she's at the end of it."

"Wow. Well, that's some motivation for you," Zillael says, which makes Fawn and I chuckle.

Zillael looks confused. She wasn't attempting to be funny, but who would've ever thought to put our life's mission into that perspective?

"What a warped female rendition of the Oedipus complex," I say while simmering down.

"Not to mention daddy complexes," Fawn adds.

"You mean the king who gouged his eyes out after getting it on with his mother?" Zillael asks, still trying to keep up with us.

"That would be him," I say.

"Really? We're like that?" Zillael frowns to really think about. "Oh my gosh, we are…"

Fawn and I burst out into laughter again.

---

It's three forty-five p.m. under the veil of the House of Benel, only minutes away from sunrise beyond our protection. I've put on a pair of thick trousers, a sturdy pair of tie-up shoes, and a thick black sweater. I advised my sisters, the only climate-sensitive beings in the group, to wear warm clothes in case they find themselves outside of my shield of warmth.

Baron has taken his sleek attire down fifty notches, but he manages to look just as debonair in a pair of black trousers and a navy blue T-shirt. He's built like a lean athlete. Before heading off to the rendezvous spot, Baron makes one of his dagger holsters into a waist-strap with a pouch for me to carry the leaf in. It's not that comfortable, but it's not uncomfortable either.

We're out in the forest, all of us, waiting for the sun to rise in the real world. I still have a slight issue with Zillael's style. She's wearing those baggy overalls over a thick red sweater and those dreadful brown work boots. I'm not a fashionista, but what a person wears says a lot about how they feel. Normally, I wouldn't concern myself with what a person wears, but I want her happy, exuberant, over the moon. It dawns on me that we all have to recover from the life we lived before we knew who we truly are. After everything I've been through, I understand why I had to be hidden from the Evil. Hopefully one day soon, Zillael will feel the same way.

"You have everything?" Lorenzo says, appearing beside me. I didn't see the butterfly fly in.

"If you mean the leaf"—I pat the side of my waist—"I have it."

Then lo and behold, Viesel Egos shows up. Zillael's and Vayle's eyes fall over him as their mouths part in awe.

"He's like that guy," Vayle whispers to Zillael.

Before she can reply, "that guy" shows up. He has blue eyes like Viesel Egos, but his skin is the same shade Raz (my childhood nanny's boyfriend) would turn after two months of surfing in the California sun.

"Cleotis Lux," Derek greets him.

Cleotis Lux nods at him. His temperament is much like Viesel Egos's. Zillael eyes turn watery as she stares at him. His arrival changes her entire demeanor. I want to tune into her and feel what's going on with her, but I can't at the moment.

"You know the way?" Viesel Egos asks me as another person shows up.

I can hardly concentrate with so much going on. "Yes." My eyes shift to the new guy.

Viesel Egos touches my temples. Baron instantly watches closely. After about five seconds, Viesel Egos drops his arms, puts his hands in his jacket, and waits. Fawn stares at the new man as if she's seeing a ghost, and he stares at her just the same.

I walk over to her and put a hand on her shoulder. "Who is he?"

"Titus Rona."

"Who's that?"

She swallows hard. She glances at Lorenzo, who's studying her. "He's my Viesel Egos."

"Falu," Titus Rona says in the same mundane tone Viesel Egos uses.

"I thought Lario killed him," I whisper.

"Me too," she whispers back.

"Another thing he lied about."

"I guess so." She's grinning and looks so happy that I go inside of her. She feels safer with a sense of normalcy returning to her.

Titus Rona is the color of milk, and the brows above his eyes are the same color as his skin. He looks ghostly with those royal blue eyes; I've never seen eyes that color. It's so funny that we're all creatures made by the hand of God. I've always known that our differences are His beautiful artwork on display. That's why I went to that lecture nine years ago, *God the First Sculptor*, given by Dr. Dove, who I now know as Lario Exgesis. That was the night I first saw Baron. Looking at these three men, and the Weks, and my sisters and me, proves my hypothesis.

The sun will rise very soon. I look at our group. Baron is chatting with Lorenzo. He and the Wek are becoming friends or something, which is good, I think. I never did ask what they were looking for in those books. Vayle is speaking to Zillael, whose eyes keep darting over to Derek. She keeps laughing softly, wearing a weak smile whenever Vayle says something amusing. I'm sure she'd laugh more if Derek didn't distract her. Derek just stands off alone, avoiding looking toward Zillael. Fawn's arm is wrapped around mine. She's smiling more than she has since returning to Earth.

Finally, she lets go of my arm and approaches Titus Rona. "How have you been?"

"Would you like me to say I've been well, Falu?" he asks, which is amusing because it's something that Viesel Egos would ask me if I asked him the same question.

"Have you?"

"I guess. Yes, I have."

"Where have you been all of these years?"

"Waiting," he answers.

"Waiting where?"

"Waiting," he snaps.

And that's the end of their conversation.

In only a few minutes, the sun will make an appearance. I sigh to calm my nerves, and Baron darts over to stand by my side.

"Maybe I should look for Lario before we head out to see if he's set up a trap for us or something," I suggest.

But Viesel Egos hears me just as the tip of the sun appears. "No need to. The evil knows you have the power of sun. It knows where you're going." He looks up. "Cover me and the rest with the veil."

He sounds as demanding as ever, but I've grown accustomed to his tone. I trust that I must do as I'm told because in these circumstances, he certainly knows what's best. I take from the protection splayed over the property and spread it over Viesel Egos first and then rest of us. He nods and faces forward.

Still glaring at the day ahead of us, he says, "Let's go," and charges off, confident that we will follow.

I take Baron's hand. Vayle steps in front of us, Zillael beside him, and they step out into the dawn. Derek trails them. Baron looks at me. I lift my brows, resolved to follow through with what was, until yesterday, the impossible. Together we enter the cold morning. Lorenzo and Fawn move out behind us. The two celestial guardians are the last to leave the forest of the House of Benel.

We're heading north toward the Canadian border. I've created the shield of invisibility and made both of my sisters warm like I promised. Everyone's silent. Baron can't keep his eyes off the ground, at last able to view the world in the daylight.

*Move ahead of us; we need your eyes*, Viesel Egos says in my head.

I do exactly as I'm told. I use my ability to go out of myself and ahead of the group.

For hours, we soar in the air, climbing higher and then dropping lower as the terrain changes. The farther north we go, the icier the ground turns. We pass snow-coated mountains, valleys of thick white ice outlining the seacoast. I'm searching for fog, but the air around and ahead of us is crystal clear.

Since I'm alone really, I check out what's happening on the ground. I see a pack of wolves chasing down a bison. The hefty animal gallops across the icy highland, kicking up snow, while the wild dogs jump and bite at it. It's a savage scene, and I can't believe I'm privy to it. My instincts to preserve life kick in. I want to help the trapped bison, but then a part of me asks, *What about the wolves?*

However, the strangest thing happens. All of a sudden, the seven wolves pull back and the bison hobbles to a stop. The chase is over. The animal's hooves shuffle its massive body around. It stares down the pack of ravenous wolves. They bark, snarl, and snap their teeth but refuse to cross the invisible line separating them. After facing them, the bison limps away.

Only then do I realize that I stopped to take in this spectacle. It means something, and I move on, attempting to figure out what that is. Another hour passes and then another. Maybe this road *isn't* as dangerous as Felix said it would be. At least we aren't running into any vampires.

I open my ears to hear what's going on in the group. Baron still holds my hand tightly. He knows I'm not fully there. The guardians are spaced around the group. Cleotis Lux holds up the rear. Titus Rona takes the middle. Baron gazes ahead, hoping to get a glimpse of me in this state. Zillael and Vayle are shooting the breeze.

"I'd sit down with a glass of cold milk and a whole plate of hot, chewy chocolate chip cookies," Vayle says with a far-off look in his eyes.

Zillael smiles amused. "You really miss home, don't you?"

"I miss my mom," he whispers so low that only Zillael can hear him.

"What kind of mother do you have?"

"Had, you mean."

"Is she dead?"

Vayle stops visualizing his mother. "No."

"Then I mean *have*."

"My mom is sweet, and not in the cliché way. She's actually sweet." He grins nostalgically. "When I was eight or nine, she made me wear this green stocking cap."

"Pretty color." Zillael grins at him.

"It was dark green," he says in his own defense.

"Oh, well that makes a difference."

"Just listen, Zill."

"I'm listening."

"No, you were being funny."

"I'm not funny."

He grunts a throaty laugh. "I know you're not. Just listen. I'm telling you about my mom. Jeez."

She sighs. "Oh my goodness, just tell me then."

"Okay, so on snowy days, she wanted me to keep my head warm, said it kept the 'snotty monster' away. I'm eight, and she's calling a cold 'the snotty monster.' But I didn't care, you know; she's my mom. And every time I left the damn cap at home, she'd chase the bus down. But she never came empty-handed. She'd bring the rest of the cookies she'd made that morning for the kids and the bus driver. I'd leave that hat home at least twice a week. Not on purpose, but it did make me popular." He sniffs a chuckle.

Zillael smiles. "That sounds like the mother I always wanted."

"All my friends wanted her too. But she was mine."

"*Is* yours," Zillael corrects.

They beam at each other.

"Do you think when all this is over, I'll be…" He doesn't finish.

"Human again?" Zillael finishes for him.

"Yes?"

She narrows her eyes inquisitively at my body. "I don't know, but Clarity would. She knows everything."

He glances at me. "Yeah, but she's so damn serious. I'm scared of her and Thor." He whispers the last part, hoping Baron doesn't hear him.

Zillael laughs out loud, so Baron looks at them

anyway. So does everyone else, except the guardians.

She covers her mouth and giggles. "Sorry."

Derek struggles not to let the moments Zillael is sharing with Vayle bother him. I think Zillael is still very hurt by Derek, but she's got Vayle. He's giving her no time to feel the ache.

I can't believe we've traveled so many hours. I really want to rejoin the group. I want all of me to be next to Baron. He's so close but so far at the same time. I'm just about to ask Viesel Egos if I can return to myself when I see something up ahead.

It's not fog. It's swirling ice and wind. I report the sight to Viesel Egos.

*Come back*, he commands.

I'm sort of relieved but also alarmed. As soon as I'm one hundred percent me, Baron draws me into him.

"Glad you're back," he says.

"We're coming up on something that looks like a blizzard," I tell him.

"Stop," Viesel Egos calls out.

We all pull up to a grinding halt.

"Falu, you won't be able to force the storm away, so clear a path through it." Then he looks at Baron and me. "Cl'auta, Ze Feldis, give us light."

I stare at him, confused. I "love" the way Viesel Egos spouts out all of these orders, assuming we can snap to it without really understanding how. I mean, can Baron and I just generate light whenever we want? I thought we could only use it to directly battle the evil or to fill me with it. I had no idea we could just shoot it out whenever we chose.

As Baron and I stare at each other, Viesel orders us all to move out. I look at Fawn, who shrugs. She lifts her palm, and I can see her power of force swirling in a cylinder shape ahead of us. The closer we get to the storm, the more I see why we need light. Although the ice is white, the path through it is pitch-black. Baron and I lift our arms and aim our palms toward the opening Fawn carved out. It all seems to be working.

"Whoa!" Vayle says, but he can't marvel for long.

"Zillael, Vayle, up front," Viesel Egos says as, one by one, we enter the gap. "Be ready for battle."

Zillael turns back to look at Fawn and me with wide eyes.

*He wouldn't put you there if you couldn't handle it*, I say.

*We won't let anything happen to you*, Fawn adds.

Zillael's eyes are still wide. I need to know how

scared she is, so I check. Her heart is beating fast; she's having a minor panic attack. She wants to run home to Moonridge, promising to never complain about high school or the people in it again.

I want to throw my arms around her and tell her to find the courage within her, but I can't. *Derek? Zillael!*

Without a word, he darts to her side. They gaze at each other.

"Losing your edge?" he asks with a smile.

She gives him a side-eyed glance and frowns. "You're talking to me *now?*"

"And where's *my* pep talk?" Vayle chimes in.

Viesel looks over his shoulder to shush them. I think he's more irritated than worried about our safety.

*Cl'auta*, Viesel says, *make your own protection. Felix Benel's power doesn't work here.*

I only have seconds to figure out what Viesel Egos is talking about. Then I do something I've never done before—encase Felix's protection. I need to know what it consists of.

I've become matter. I'm solid. I hear nothing, but I see everything. I'm an impenetrable shield. A purple evening is not too far ahead.

I do my best to replicate what my father

created. I come back into myself, and my eyes are pinned to Zillael and Vayle. Never have I worried about putting so much faith into this ability of mine. They exit the tunnel, the first to walk into the night sky under my version of Felix's protection. So far they're facing no aggression. Viesel Egos's sword isn't even drawn, which is the best sign that all is clear.

We're all out, and Fawn's tunnel vanishes. Ice covers the ground in the form of loose snow and solid chunks. Frozen mountain ranges tower over the valleys, and I can't see the coast in the distance anymore. There's nothing here—no trees and very few rocks. I've never seen so much ice in my life.

"Where is this place, Egos?" I ask.

"Nowhere," he answers.

"Do you mean this place is called *Nowhere?*"

"Yes."

I'm scanning the ground, looking for something. It's night, and according to the Script, we're to travel during the day. I never thought we would take this long to get this far, and according to the directions inside me, we have a while to go before arriving at the Box of Jari. So I'm looking for our accommodations. Felix surely wouldn't send us out here without an appropriate place to lodge, would he?

"No traveling at night, right?" Baron says.

I'm still searching below. "Yeah. But…"

"We should camp here," Fawn says.

"Camp?" I'm stunned. I hadn't considered that.

Fawn chuckles. "Never camped before, Cl'auta?"

"No, can't say that I have."

"What about you, Zillael?"

Zillael nods stiffly. "Once." She's not happy with the idea either. She and I are in the same frame of mind. We both want to be anywhere but here.

"Well, don't worry." Fawn pats what looks like a satchel that's slung over her shoulder. "I have us covered."

I squint at the bag, wondering what she has in it. It's not big enough for a tent. I hadn't even noticed it until she touched it—that's how small it is.

"Well, we have to stop now," I say loud enough for Viesel to hear. "I guess we'll have to wait out the night somewhere…." I look over the land again. "Down there."

Baron points to spot below. "Egos!"

Viesel Egos's eyes follow Baron's finger. Once he

sees where Baron is leading us, he shoots toward that ground. Once again, we all follow.

We settle down for the night in a cozy space between three gigantic boulders. It feels so dangerous out here. We watch Fawn blow the snow clear from the ground. The force of her wind actually dries the soil, and she even builds walls that rise about ten feet around the perimeter, behind the boulders. Then she opens the satchel bag that hangs on her hip and takes out three tightly rolled mats.

She tosses one to Zillael and me. "Spread them on the ground."

"Done this much?" I ask as I unravel mine.

"Many times." She winks at me.

For the final touch, she breaks two yellow light sticks and sets them in the middle of the circle that everyone but the guardians sits in. Viesel Egos, Cleotis Lux, and Titus Rona stomp off in different directions across the frozen terrain.

We're sitting on the ground with our backs against the hard boulders. When I shift to find a more comfortable position, Baron places me between his legs. I sigh with relief as I rest my back against his chest.

"Where did you get all of this stuff from?" I ask Fawn

She's lying on the ground, gazing up at the cloudy sky with a nostalgic gleam in her eyes. "I used to live like this. For about a hundred years, once."

"Really?" I say as Zillael says, "Wow!"

"Can't be true. You're what, twenty-five years old?" Vayle asks.

She looks at Vayle. "Three hundred or so, but I'm not counting anymore." Then she looks between Zillael and me. "Yeah, I just didn't want to be part of society during those years. Humans know how to reach their all-time low, and they do it often. Maybe if I had Cl'auta's power, I would've stuck around."

"Why my ability?" I ask.

"Maybe if I had more insight to why people are the way they are, I could excuse their behavior."

"Well, what happened?" I ask.

It looks as if Fawn is staring at me, but she's actually looking past me. "Hate happened. Humans can really manifest that word and become very dangerous. I couldn't even be seen with my own father." She shakes her head. "I couldn't be part of those people."

"I understand," Baron says out of nowhere.

"A hundred years," Vayle ponders out loud. "And you guys aren't vampires?"

Zillael says, "Are we ever going to get old and die?"

"Gosh, I hope so," I mutter. I feel Baron stiffen.

"Me too," Vayle chimes in. "I never got the whole thing with living forever. You do your time, and then you're done."

"I agree," I say. "I never thought I'd live for three hundred years, let alone thousands. I think people are afraid of death for no reason. I was never afraid."

"Why not?" Vayle asks.

"Because if everyone has to do it, then it must not be that bad. People fear it because there are so many narratives about what happens after you die. My narrative has always been—I'll see when I get there."

We fall silent, which is deafening in this place called Nowhere. There's no wind, no leaves rustling or water moving. It's just silent.

"You know what I miss?" Zillael whispers, still looking far off. "Candy apples."

Derek half smiles. "Jake's?"

She smiles at him and nods. Now they're sharing a moment. Vayle squeezes her thigh—his hand is very high up her leg—but that's not enough to distract her.

"Hey," Baron whispers in my ear.

"Hey…"

"You don't want to live forever with me?"

"Of course I do. Why would you ask me that?"

"Because of what you said."

"Oh." I pause, choosing my words carefully. "If I have to live forever, I want to live forever with you. But…" I hesitate, trying to explain. "I've been hearing thoughts and feeling emotions from others since I was a kid. Life is a roller coaster. One day you're happy, the next you're not. Something or someone will eventually throw a wrench into your happiness."

"I'll never let that happen to us," Baron promises.

"I know." And I truly believe he'd do anything to keep me happy. "I used to think I was human, and I wasn't happy, Baron. Not really. You changed that when you came back into my life." I let out a soft laugh. "I mean, sure, a stranger nearly killed me, and your psychotic vampire ex stabbed me, but I met Adore, then Fawn, and I fell in love with you. Now I have Zillael too. So, yeah, I'm happy now. But can you imagine watching humans give in to evil for another hundred years? I don't want to hear it or feel it for another day, let alone a century."

Baron kisses the side of my face. "Well, Cl'auta…"

I grin. "Speaking Enuian, are we?"

He chuckles, then turns serious. "Didn't you tell me you saved two human lives just yesterday?"

"Yes," I reply, curious where he's heading with this.

"How did that make you feel?"

That's a good question. I venture back to feel the moments when I saved the girl Lario wanted to turn and the girl he wanted to kill. "Needed, I guess."

"And when we are together," he whispers, "how does it feel?"

I hum, grinning like I'm floating through rainbow clouds. "You know how it feels."

"The call of duty and the call of love. You have to admit our forever will be kind of fun."

I lift my face to look at him, and his lips consume mine.

"Just wanted to let you know we can hear and see you," Vayle says in his usual cynically playful way.

When I join Baron in giving him a stern look,

he lifts his hands in mock surrender. "It's all good. I'm only saying—it *sounded* like a private moment, but it wasn't."

"It was beautiful," Zillael can barely say. She sounds all choked up.

Fawn grins from ear to ear. "It was like watching *The Young and the Restless.*"

We all laugh, even the Weks. As the hours pass, we learn a lot about each other. For instance, Zillael has no plans—no college plans, no career plans, not even leisure plans.

"So what are you going to do after you graduate from high school?" I ask.

"I'm going back to high school?" she asks.

"Don't you think you need a diploma?"

She shrugs. "I kind of want to do what Falu did. You know, live in the wilderness for a hundred years. If I can do that, that's what I'll do."

"Really?" Vayle asks, shocked. "Not me."

"What will you do with a hundred years?" I ask him.

"I already said I don't want to live a hundred years. I meant it."

"Well, I do," Zillael counters, a bit snippety.

"Well, I don't," Vayle says.

"I didn't ask you to."

"Well don't because I won't."

"I tell you what," Fawn cuts in. "Zillael, when the time comes to escape humanity, I'll take you with me." She winks at her.

Zillael's entire face lights up. "And I'm going."

Derek can't stop himself from smiling at Zillael. He's over the moon for her. I wonder if a Wek can be fully in love with a Life Blood. I'll have to ask Lorenzo.

Fawn tells us all about living in the wild. Animals weren't afraid of her, and when the weather got too extreme, she'd simply move to another place. She used to return home to Enu for meals with Felix. Sometimes her stay there made the years pass faster on Earth.

"What does Enu look like?" Zillael asks.

"Probably like heaven," I reply. "But you'll see for yourself."

"I will?"

"Yes, you will."

"Hell, can I go too?" Vayle asks. "Since I was planning on going to heaven anyway."

Fawn and I stare at him with faint, tight-lipped smiles.

"Only beings who are made from the soil of the universe can survive in Enu," Derek answers.

"So what is it?" He turns to Zillael. "You're from this Enu place?"

"Apparently."

"And you're going back there, and I'm going to be here all by myself? What about you?" He stabs Derek with his eyes. "Are you from Ono or Enu too?"

"Oh, calm down, Vayle," Zillael barks. "No one's leaving you anywhere by yourself. Just have hope, right?" She looks at Fawn. "That's what you told me. We have hope that we all get what we want when this is over." She turns back to Vayle. "Even you."

After another awkward span of silence, I mention how Fawn took an active part in the women's suffrage movement.

"And civil rights," she adds. "Then I was a hippie for a while…"

"For a while?" Vayle says. "You mean for a hundred years, right? Living in the bushes? That's totally some hippie crap. And speaking of crap, what did you do for that?"

Zillael rolls her eyes and shakes her head. "Don't ask a girl anything like that. Come on…"

"My goodness, you two are like an old cranky

married couple." Fawn laughs. "But Zillael is right. Don't ask me that."

"Okay," Vayle complains. Of course, he takes another swipe at Zillael, asking her how she expected to make it in the world without college.

We have to hear that verbal battle for about ten minutes, which ends with Vayle asking me if I went to college since I have the Power of Mind.

"I bet you did, right?" he asks.

I sigh because I don't want to be dragged into their spat. "Yes." I mutter regardless.

"See?" he says, sounding victorious.

"Just shut up," Zillael barks.

"How about we play who can be quietest the longest?" Baron says, staring daggers at Vayle.

"Got it," Vayle says, realizing he's the only participant in that game.

Three hours pass. Despite all of their bickering, Vayle and Zillael roll up into each other to sleep. Derek sits across from them, staring shamelessly at her face.

Fawn and Lorenzo are having a conversation about all the types of animals she's run into over the years. It sounds as if he's just trying to keep her talking. He asks all the questions and listens attentively as she explains what an anteater looks like up close. He says something that sticks in my mind though: all of these years, he never paid attention to what animals looked like because they don't pose a threat to the daughters of the House of Benel. There are no animals in Enu, which Fawn and I already knew. What strikes me is how truly singular the Wek's, and even the guardians', mission in life is. Maybe ours should be just as singular—fulfill the prophecy of the Script. Maybe that's why Zillael couldn't come up with any future plans. Deep down, her Enuian and divine sides know that this is it.

As Falu explains how she lived in Madagascar before it become popular for tourists, I lie on top of Baron. His body is the perfect mattress.

"Well, this was a fun night," he says sarcastically.

I chuckle a little. "If Zill and Vayle were married, they'd be divorced in two years."

"You mean two months."

We laugh.

I set my chin on his chest to look into those bottomless eyes of his. "I love you."

"You can never love me more than I love you, Clarity. I'll die without you. You can't say that."

I think about Adore, Fawn, and Zillael.

"Thinking about your sisters?" he asks with a smile.

I realize I just looked off, which I do when I'm pondering something. "Yeah." I pull my mouth into a frown.

He kisses my lips. "Don't. I love that you have your sisters."

"But you have them too," I say. "Fawn loves you. And I forgot to tell you this, but Adore told me to tell you thank you. Oh, and Viesel Egos too."

"Hey, how can you forget that?" he teases.

We laugh quietly and kiss some more. But we decide to do what's good for the both of us and not begin something that will take privacy to finish.

Before sunrise, I learn that Baron is still rich from old money. When his father learned that Baron was a vampire, he used it to the Ze Feldis clan's advantage. When I asked him how, Baron promised to tell me one day. However, all of their wealth was left to him. The walls of Ze Feldis were eventually raided during a daylight attack, and he couldn't do anything to save his family. He got this far-off look in his eyes. I could tell he was reliving that day, so I didn't push him any further.

He just said, "They took everything, but I got it back." He then came to America, bought a lot of stuff, increased the value, and sold it. "And that's what I do still. But ever since I met you in Cambridge, I wanted to do other things."

"Like what?" I can't help but ask.

His eyes examine the world around us. "This— with you." Baron's hands slide up and down my lower back. He has a very sensual touch.

I purr and let myself taste his neck. "We don't have very long until sunrise, so why don't you sneak me around that rock over there and let's make out like crazy until then?" I kiss his lips. I feel him rising beneath me, agreeing.

In a blink of an eye, we're behind a large rock, rolling around in the snow, kissing and fondling and unable to get deep enough into each other. And just as we planned, we don't stop until sunrise.

## CHAPTER 11

# THE CURE

"Come on, Cl'auta," Fawn scolds me. "You didn't think you would get wet? And we can catch a fever, you know. I lived in Antarctica—I know." Fawn uses her power to blow my clothes dry, refusing to let me ride the wind all wet.

"Thanks," I tell her once she's done.

For general purposes, she dries Baron off too. We take off as soon as the sun rises.

"Should I move ahead of us?" I ask Viesel Egos.

"There's no need to." He gives me a side-eyed glance. "Stay alert."

The sun is out in full about two hours into our journey. The farther we go, the more the snow melts, giving way to dry lands. I remove the warm shield from myself to test the temperature. It's still ice-cold.

Also, the sky still holds pockets of soot-colored clouds. They're lower now and becoming scarce as we gain ground. Black ash-heaps are plastered across the terrain. If we weren't alert before, we are now. There's an ominous feeling in the air, which causes me to open up. We're being watched, but whatever or whoever it is keeps its distance.

"Get ready," escapes my lips as I gaze over the land.

Derek shoots up to Zillael's side. I feel Baron's entire body snap into high alert. I'm sure there's a story about him being a soldier, maybe a mercenary, somewhere in the three hundred-plus years he's lived.

I flow out of myself to mix with the dead air that surrounds us. I'm trying to get to the higher hills in the distance. I suspect that whatever's stalking us is hiding behind them. If I can get a glimpse of our would-be aggressors, then maybe we can be better prepared to fight them. There's going to be a fight for sure. But I'm not making much headway because I'm besieged by a familiar energy. It's red, like blood. Lario tapped into this power the first time he stopped me from discovering his whereabouts. I know what I need to overpower it, and I can reach for Baron's hand.

Lorenzo shouts, *Get back now!*

Alarmed, I do as I'm told. Chaos has broken out all around me. Fawn has created a wall of wind around me that keeps what's attacking me at bay. Each time one of the black, shadowy creatures—which are ashes in the form of human beings—flies toward me, the wind from the shield rips it apart, sending it whimpering away as it disintegrates. Baron fights beside my capsule, working with those two blades of his. He swipes at two, sometimes three, shadow monsters at a time.

Zillael moves just as quickly as Baron. Her fighting is graceful, and instincts drive her motions. As her hands and feet connect with the creatures, she detaches their shadowy heads or tears holes right through their hearts. It seems she's attacking those two areas precisely—the head and heart. Derek and Vayle, who fight just as hard as Zillael, are using the same technique. The guardians expertly wield their swords of fire, and I can't see Lorenzo anywhere.

We form a formidable army of a few, but I know what it will take to get rid of these things. I activate the light within me and push it out. I envision Baron's light, hoping it will allow me to take from him without touching him. It seems to work. I see both of our energies swirling in my head. Felix once instructed me to keep my eyes open when I use my abilities, and now I know why.

When I open my eyes, I see that the light is trapped inside the capsule Fawn created around me. *Fawn*, I shout in her head, *release me!*

After she takes a quick glance at me to confirm that I'm fully back, the shield evaporates. The light explodes all around us. We freeze in place but stay on guard as the shadowy beings wither into ashes, mixing with the soot already on the ground. They don't die silently; they cry out like banshees in excruciating pain.

Soon we're all alone again, looking at each other, wondering what in the world just happened.

"I told you to stay here," Viesel Egos reprimands me.

I look at him. "I'm sorry." I turn to all the flustered faces and shake my head. "Really, I'm sorry."

"You don't have to apologize," Baron says, narrowing his eyes at Viesel Egos. "We all have responsibilities here, and we held our ground. Didn't we?" He glares at everyone, demanding to be backed up by every single person in the group.

It takes them a moment to shake off the shock of what just happened, but one by one, he gets what he expects.

"But what the hell was that?" Vayle asks, still dazed. "That was stuff you see in video games. But that was real!"

"Is this also part of Nowhere?" I ask Viesel Egos.

"Yes," he answers.

Lorenzo the butterfly flutters through the air and transforms back into his human form. "This wasn't created by the Creator. So technically, it's Nowhere."

"Where did you go?" I ask him.

"I can only be aggressive when you choose might as your weapon," he replies.

"I see." I understand him completely. "So this is not part of Earth's universe?"

"Not even close. But what you just faced is only the beginning. It knows where you're going." Lorenzo studies us all with eyes of doom. "It wants all of you dead, but right now, one of you more than the others."

We all look at each other, wondering who that might be. All eyes settle on me. I guess I would be the obvious choice.

"The Selell with the power of the sun," Lorenzo says.

All of our eyes snap toward Vayle.

"Me?" He gulps, looking frightened out of his mind.

"Don't worry, Vayle," Zillael says to comfort him. "We won't let anything happen to you."

But he frowns harder. I can see what's motivating him to continue on—his human life. He truly wants the opposite of what Lario gave up his decency to change. Vayle is a vampire who only wants to be human again. My senses perk up. I feel something brewing from miles out. Lorenzo is right; we're in the thick of it. Danger lurks in every direction, and it has us in its sights.

"We should keep moving," I say. My voice sounds shaky. The longer we wait, the stronger the energy gets.

Viesel Egos nods. We all do what we have to do to regroup. For me, that means taking a deep sigh. Together, we take to the sky.

Our mouths remain closed, but our eyes are open, scoping out the ground and the space around us. About an hour later, the valley of ashes transforms into a dry, cracked terrain. It's a desolate canyon that goes on forever. The soil is a dead orange color, and that same toxic hue is trapped in the air. I'm almost afraid to breathe it.

"Give me what belongs to me and live. Take it and die," a voice hisses like a snake.

We all look at each other, trying to figure out where it came from.

"And I'm taking Ze Feldis too," it says.

Without hesitation, Baron pulls his daggers. "Come get me."

I glance at him and do a double take. I've never seen him so incensed. I have no idea what's fueling the fire in him.

All the light cuts off, as if someone flipped a switch. It's pitch-black. In the darkness, I hear everyone say, "What the hell?" or "What?" or a combination of both. I feel the opposition moving into their ranks, increasing in number. There's a loud howling. Even if we tried to speak, we wouldn't be able to hear each other.

*Zill, Vayle, both of you call out the sun*, I say in their heads. I feel hesitation from both of them. *Now!*

The two who hold the power of the sun activate their ability. On the horizon to the north and west, two suns rise. One is yellow; one is red. We all gawk as the orange day returns with a vengeance. Its heat scalds the earth, causing smoke to rise. It would be enough to kill my sisters and me if my shields didn't hold. The deafening noise has come to a halt. I feel the strength of our adversary dwindling.

Zillael and Vayle stare at each other thinking, *What just happened?*

Viesel Egos and the other guardians have their swords drawn. I think he's about to give us the order to move out, but he rushes over right in front of me.

"I know what's ahead," he says. "I can't go with you farther than Nowhere. But the three daughters of the House of Benel and their Selells are strong enough for Jari."

"Wait," I say. "What about Derek and Lorenzo?"

"The Weks can't go."

"No, we can't," Lorenzo agrees.

"Why not?" I don't get it.

"We're not made from the dust of the Earth."

"You mean human?"

"We're not flesh and blood, Cl'auta. But you and your sisters have some humanity, and the Selells were once men."

I frown. I have a bunch of questions to ask, and they're coming so fast I don't know which to ask first.

"Clarity," Baron says close to my ear, "we'll be fine."

I close my eyes, sigh, and touch his chest as a reminder that we still have his strength. "I know."

"Get to the Box of Jari and open it." Lorenzo's eyes fall over all of us. "Falu, Cl'auta, Zillael, Ze Feldis, Vayle: When the gate opens, enter and it will close. You have the leaf, Cl'auta. You'll know what to do with it."

"That's what I keep hearing," I mutter.

"Where will you go?" Fawn asks him.

He stares into her eyes. "I'll return to the House of Benel."

"What about you?" Zillael asks Derek.

"I'll be there too."

"Good," she whispers.

Fawn does a better job of hiding her reaction from Lorenzo. But Derek frowns because his heart is betraying his vow. He puts his eyes on a safer subject—me.

"We'll stand with you until you all enter Jari," Derek says. "We can go with you to the gate, but that's it."

"Okay," I whisper.

There's no doubt that it's time. I have no idea what we're about to face, but I know it's no small foe. I want to move ahead to get a view of our opponents, but I'll do as I'm told. Viesel Egos has already proven that he knows more than I do about how to best defeat our enemy. He's been with us during all the pivotal fights, leading us and standing on the front lines. Now he's leaving us, and I don't know how I feel about that. Maybe a tiny bit stripped of my armor—the breastplate.

"All right, Viesel Egos, you know the way," I say.

Without hesitation, he takes off, Viesel Egos-style, and we're all forced to keep up.

Baron wraps his arm around my waist before we go. "I need to kiss you before all hell breaks loose."

I press my hand to the side of his face and my lips to his. We share a gentle, quick kiss. I think about how much I love him, and I hope to God not to lose him during this leg of the journey. My heart flutters, the light in me is stirred up, and when I open my eyes, I see that his face is aglow and so is mine.

"Ready?" he asks.

"Ready."

A half-mile ahead, the flat, brittle landscape comes to an abrupt end. Heavy breathing, throaty growls, and teeth gnashing fill the air. It's the sound of hungry, angry beasts.

"Everybody keep your head; know your strength," Baron says, taking over like a colonel leading his injured general's squad into battle.

The guardians engage their swords. Baron clutches his daggers. Fawn and I stand together in the center of the circle the others have formed around us. Lorenzo joins us this time. I'm curious to see what powers he has to contribute. Whatever his powers, they must be similar to my own. Derek has taken on Zillael's abilities, so I assume Lorenzo has mine. I'll keep my eyes on him.

"Daughters of Felix Benel," Viesel Egos shouts over his shoulder. It's the loudest I've ever heard him speak. "You *must* kill. These are not creatures made by the hand of God. Kill!"

My sisters and I look at each other. It is a reminder that deep within ourselves, we have the drive to preserve life, not take it. The way I want Lario Exgesis dead is unnatural.

Viesel Egos looks at all the guardians and lastly at Baron. Without another word, he shoots off toward the cliff. What's over the hill is getting closer, and my shields are being attacked. I'm straining to hold up the shield I created from Felix's protection. I pull light from Baron. It helps a little, but I'll have to take more to maintain it, and I don't want to deplete him. The closer we get, the more flustered I become.

We shoot over the cliff. There's another dry valley below, and cutting through the middle of it is a narrow gulf so deep I cannot perceive the bottom of it.

"It's an abyss," Lorenzo says to Fawn and me.

On each side of the fissure are thousands of creatures, possibly millions. I recoil because they're nasty-looking. A number of them are patched together with dead body parts—arms, legs, bodies, and heads that don't match. Some have bulbous heads made of mounds of rotted flesh. A number of them are frail, with no muscle or meat, just skin around bone. I'm repulsed, but the disgust passes and is replaced by pity. I take on their pain. It hurts to be them, I mean physically hurts.

Viesel Egos wastes no time guiding us onto a smooth surface set before a wall of solid orange rock. It extends high in the air. Already some of these beings are scampering up the wall like ants on candy. As we advance, they jump at us. Swords of fire and silver blades cut them down. The way Zillael fights is unreal. She's so swift that her moves can't be followed by the eye. She's pulling the creatures apart limb by limb, and so are Vayle and Derek. They fight like an army of thirty thousand.

At the same time, Lorenzo shoots light at the beings. The beams invade them and send them jumping into the pitch-black gorge. Their screeching is deafening as they leap, escaping the agony the light causes. I know my light will clear them out, but when I push it out, a force limits the scope of the impact.

One of the monsters climbs onto Baron's back, and out of sheer horror, I push the light hard out of my hands. The patched-up creature glows from head to toe before leaping head-first into the pit. Light gushes from my palms now. I take out an entire section of these patched-up people, sending thousands of them back to hell.

I realize that the force that's been working to limit my powers was prevailing because I haven't yet truly dedicated myself to the fight. That was what Viesel Egos's warning was all about. I cannot over-whelm the Evil if I want to preserve its life. They must go, and I must get to the Box of Jari.

I see Zillael take a hit to the stomach. She bends over to absorb the impact. When the creature reaches out to grab her head, I dig all the way down to my toes and push every piece of light I can access out of me. I keep my eyes open as the blinding rays engulf us. The Evil tries to fight back, but I'm too strong for it. I draw from the last thing I saw—the monster with my sister's head between its mismatched hands. I remember how its filthy, sharp fingernails cut into the skin of her beautiful cheeks.

The creature has been forced to let go of Zillael and jumped back into the pit. She's bleeding, and though I want to stop and tend to her injuries, I don't. None of us stop advancing. Our attackers leap back into the darkness, but the Evil hasn't let up on me.

The Box of Jari calls me to it. My eyes rest on a glowing yellow spot high up on the rock wall. As I lift myself up, a force pushes down on my shoulders and head. I strain against it, clenching my teeth and grunting. I make little headway, but then Baron sees me struggling. He rushes over and puts his head between my legs, hoisting me up on his shoulders. Although the force continues to fight me, it's no match for Baron's strength. I'm only focused on the yellow light, and we approach it at a pretty fast speed. This is no cakewalk for Baron either.

"Here!" I shout.

Baron stops and holds our ground. The light is in front of my nose. My instincts tell me to press my right hand over it—not left but *right*—and I do it. Instantly, a shadow falls over the land. The weight lifts off my shoulders, and the ground rumbles.

"Go!" Viesel Egos shouts.

I look up. At the very top of the wall, right above my head, a doorway is aglow. Baron sees it too. In one swift movement, I'm no longer on his shoulders. His arms are wrapped around me, and we shoot up toward the entry. A yellow pillow of light engulfs me for a few seconds, and then it's over. We're on the ground, surrounded by more desolation.

Between the icebox we camped in last night, the ash land where we faced off with the black shadows, and the valley of cracked rock that regurgitated creatures from hell, this place is by far the worst. Spiny trees made up of gray branches and charred tree trunks coat the earth as far as the eye can see. The sky is dark gray, but there's a sheet of white hidden behind it. That provides us with enough light to see where we're going. None of this looks real. It looks like a movie set where the air is still, the sky is violet, and the forest is dead.

I'm uneasy, so my senses are picking up energies. One thing's for sure; we're not alone. They're all looking at me, Zillael, Fawn, Vayle, and Baron. I hug myself, the way I used to comfort myself years ago. It feels like I haven't embraced myself like this in a long time. My eyes give our surroundings another once-over. I break out in chills.

"This place gives me the creeps," I say.

All I want is to be in bed with Baron. I want to carry out our plans to make love at the Ashford Castle in Cong, Ireland and explore the canals of Amsterdam on his gondola. He promised to show me how to dance the night away in some of the trendiest nightclubs in Paris. I want to cry because I know my wishful thinking is just that.

Baron takes my hand, which stops me from embracing myself. "Are you okay, love?"

After I hesitate to ponder that, I drop my face and nod.

"Look at me, Clarity," he says. "If I could do all of this for you, I would. Listen… If I feel that you're frightened, I'm going to worry. If I worry, my head's not in the game. I need you to show me you're okay."

"I'm fine," I say. "I mean it."

Baron kisses my forehead.

"How about we all take a moment?" Fawn says. "Just to breathe."

That's when I remember the cut on Zillael's

face. I whip around to see her standing next to Vayle. "Where is it?"

She looks confused.

I run my fingers down the side of her face. "You were bleeding."

"Oh, yeah that. I heal fast, some times faster than others. I guess this time it was really fast."

"So if where we left was Nowhere, what's this called?" Vayle asks, scanning our surroundings.

"It's Jari, remember?" I turn my head to gaze out over it. "And I don't think we're alone here."

Everyone studies our environment. It's apparent I'm not the only one who's wary of this vast wasteland.

"Where is there to hide?" Baron asks, still looking around.

I, on the other hand, look down. "I think it's under our feet. We should keep moving." I think whatever's hunting us is doing more than following us; it's stalking us.

"But where are we going?" Zillael asks.

"Wherever this tugging inside of me leads us."

Fawn nods. "Well, if it's tugging, then we should follow."

We're all in agreement, and we attempt to lift up off the ground. Baron and Vayle lift into the air, but a force holds my sisters' and my feet to the ground.

"What?" Zillael glares at her brown boots.

"It's not an energy that's doing this. I think here we're just a little limited," I reply.

"A little?" Zillael tries to lift herself again.

"We can walk," Fawn offers as the vampires return to the ground.

"I'll carry you," Baron says to me.

I shake my head. "No. We have to walk, and all three of us have to stay together. At least, that's what I feel."

Baron watches me for a moment. I have no idea what he's looking for, but he eventually mutters, "Okay."

So we continue on at a regular pace through the truly petrified forest. At times, our feet kick up soot, and I get thirstier and hungrier as the minutes turn. I catch Baron swallowing hard. I know what he's doing. He's trying to moisten his parched throat.

We've probably gone a mile without speaking before Zillael says, "Gosh, I could really go for a Jake's candy apple."

Vayle snorts with disdain. "And you said 'good.'" He glares at Zillael.

"What are you talking about?" she asks bitingly.

"The wreck—or Wek or whatever you call him. He said he's going to go sit by the pool and wait for you to get through this hell, and you said, 'Good.'"

She shakes her head. "He didn't say that. And he's a Wek, and you know his name."

Vayle's face gets all pinched. "He can't even come here with you. But I can. That says a hell of a lot."

"What is your problem with him? You're the one that I let…" Zillael glances at Fawn and me as she decides not to finish that remark. "Just what's your problem?"

"You're never going to get over that guy, are you?"

"Why do you even care?" Zillael snaps. "All you want is your vampire antidote."

Vayle wears a sinister smile as he shakes his head. He points at his neck. "This hurts. Guess what? I'm thirsty; you're not. Yes, I want the goddamn vampire antidote. But I want you too."

Zillael looks thrown off by his confession. Fawn, Baron, and I wait for her response.

"Look at Clarity," Vayle continues. "She's with Baron, and he's a vampire. Aren't you a vampire?"

Baron just shrugs, choosing to stay out of the discussion.

"He's a vampire," Vayle concludes. "And Fawn! Her guy, the maniac, he's a vampire, right?"

It sounds as though he's asking if Lario's a vampire, but Fawn just looks at him with tightly clenched lips. I think he gets that she's not going to answer that.

"That means you're supposed to be with a vampire," he shouts.

Zillael massages her temples. "Just be quiet. You're too smart of a person to really believe what you just said."

"What do you want me to say then?"

"Don't say anything."

"I love you," he blurts.

We all stop in our tracks, taken aback.

"Why?" Zillael asks, breaking the deafening silence.

"Because."

"Because why?"

"Hey," Baron cuts in, "can you continue this discussion later? I don't know if you've forgotten, but we're in quite a predicament here."

Zillael and Vayle stare at each other. I can't tell what they're thinking. I can't read minds here, which is both a blessing and a curse. Vayle stomps ahead of us, throwing a mini-tantrum, and we all start off after him.

After we walk a couple of feet, I ask Fawn if she's able to use the power of force. She tries it, but it doesn't work. I try shooting light out my palm, and I can.

"Well, at least we have that," I say. "I think we have our secondary abilities."

"Light and sun," Baron summarizes.

We ponder that.

I glance at him. "You're thirsty?"

"Yeah," he mutters.

He takes my hand as we walk on. I hate that I'm putting him through this. Although I want to share a bit of information with everyone, I choose not to. The truth is that I have no idea where we're going. There's no map in my head, no end point. We're walking blindly, led by pure instinct. I'm thinking this when the ground rumbles. The earth opens up, happening so fast we have no time to react. Baron pushes me away from him as he and Vayle are swallowed up.

Fawn, Zillael, and I are shocked.

Baron and Vayle are gone.

The rumbling stops. My sisters and I are alone.

"Baron!" I call over and over. I drop to my

knees and shovel through the ashes with my hands. "Bring him back!"

I can feel granules being jammed under my fingernails. The ground my knees press against feels so hard. Solid. Only a fool would think she could dig through these prison walls. Fawn and Zillael take my shoulders.

"Come on, Cl'auta," Fawn urges. "All we can do now is keep going."

"No!" I shriek. I'm wailing so loud, I'm scaring myself.

"Yes!" she demands. "Get up."

I stop shuffling through the dirt. She's right. There's nothing we can do but keep going. So I slowly rise to my feet, staring into Fawn's eyes.

"I'm sorry," I say to my sisters.

"You don't have to apologize for emoting, Cl'auta. You're not a machine. Let's just keep going. We can't stop now."

I nod and then look at Zillael. "Are you okay?"

She, too, just lost someone who's close to her.

"If he's with Baron, then I think he'll be okay," she says.

I hug Zillael, and she hugs me.

I give her a final pat on the back. "Let's go, sisters."

All I can hear are our feet clomping against the ground. I've never been so hungry. Hunger comes from the human side of me, and so does not having the ability to ride the wind. I glance at my sisters. They look pretty gaunt too. I think we're all thirsty, hungry, and weary.

"How far do we have to go?" Zillael asks. She looks around nervously.

Fawn and I see them too. Shadows are passing through the skeletal trees. We increase our pace, though the faster and farther we run, the more winded I become. But we push on. Out of nowhere, we're sideswiped by one of the shadows.

I dodge it before it can hit me. "Let's get close!"

We stand in a circle with our backs pressed against each other. I look up at the bleak sky. What looks like hundreds of shadow creatures fly over our heads.

"What now?" Zillael cries.

I have one weapon, so I aim my palms at the shadows. As light floods out of my hands and strikes one of them, they all scatter, squealing as they go.

"Let's run!" I shout.

We all take off, but the shadow creatures haven't gone anywhere. I shoot light at whatever's moving beside us, although I'm not sure if my beam is connecting. But my light has put fear in them, and that's a good thing.

We run faster and faster, giving it all that we have. Zillael is the best runner out of the three of us. Her strides are strong and sure.

Without me telling her to, she steps ahead of me and shouts, "Guide me the rest of the way, Cl'auta!"

I fall back and yell, "Keep straight!"

I drop behind Fawn since I'm the one with the active weapon. Although they're gunning for me, my number one goal is to keep her safe. I'm glancing over my right shoulder, watching my back.

Zillael yells, "Stop!"

Fawn and I do just that. One more step, and we would've fallen into a gaping hole. I'm panting, trying to catch my breath, but I study the fissure. I've seen this before, or at least something like it.

"The Forest of Naught," I whisper.

"What?" Fawn asks, winded too.

Miraculously, Zillael displays no sign of being out of breath. Without saying a word, she jumps and flips, landing on her feet behind me. After a series of fighting moves, she pins one of those shadow-like creatures to the ground.

Fawn and I are shocked. Finally we get to see up

close what's been attacking us. Zillael has a death grip on its narrow neck and bony chest. The thing's eyes are white, and its sharp teeth are snapping at us.

"How are you able to do that?" I marvel, because although it's a shadow, it's like solid matter in her hands.

"Nuke it, Cl'auta!" Zillael shouts.

I hit it with light, and it squeals as it disintegrates in her hands. I know what I have to do, and I do it quickly. The shadows are congregating overhead, and we'll be tussling with them soon. I pull up my shirt and force my hands to stop shaking. I unlatch the little black pouch and take out the leaf. While my hands are busy, the shadows make their move.

"Get down!" Zillael shouts.

Fawn and I hit the dust, but Zillael is on her feet, battling the shadows like a wild woman. I lift my palm and shoot light over me to create a protective shield. I crawl forward with the leaf in the other hand. Fawn crawls behind me, staying under the light. The shadow creatures must see the leaf because they're coming for it, even at the risk of dying. They hit my light, and their ashes pour over us. But their acts of kamikaze weaken my beam.

Another shadow takes a hit at it, and then another; it's a tactic.

"Cover the leaf, Zill!" I shout.

I drag myself across the ground and reach my arm out of the shield to cast the leaf into the hole. One of the shadows tries to chase the leaf down, but the phantom bounces off an unseen force field. The creatures' squawking is deafening now.

I hear my mind opening up again. *Something's definitely happening.*

*Think "power of the sun,"* I say to Zillael.

She nods and does just that. I think of Vayle and call his name. Although I'm unable to get to him, I have to believe that I feel myself in his head.

*Call up the sun!* I shout at him.

All I—we—can do is wait. More shadows circle us, but I see a start of a new day in the distance. My heart thumps as the creatures slam into the ground and become the dust.

"Look," Fawn says, pointing up and behind us.

A series of lights are being shot into the air. Knowing exactly what's going on, I shoot light too. I drag myself to my feet just in time for Baron to wrap his arms around me.

"What happened? Where did they take you?" I cry. I'm shaking all over.

"Calm down, love," he whispers. "We're okay now."

He's covered in soot from head to toe, but I'm looking into his blood-red eyes and at his chalky skin.

"I don't understand what happened to you," I say, unable to let it go.

"We're fine, we're fine," he says.

I see Zillael hugging Vayle, who's quite shaken. He has a blank look on his face. Something happened. Something scary.

"I need my turn," Fawn says, standing next to Baron. I let him go so that she can give him a hug. "I'm so glad to see you in one piece, Ze Feldis."

There's a loud explosion. We all gaze at the sky. What was once black and harrowing is trans-forming right before our eyes. A bright yellow sun rises on the horizon, chasing away the darkness. The earth rumbles, and a massive fusion of yellow and white light gushes out of the hole. We're all blinded by it, and the light gets brighter. I feel myself lifted about three inches higher because something cushiony is growing under my feet.

A delicate wind blows the light away. The wind is soft and cool on my sweaty skin. When the world becomes visible again, we're all choked with awe.

Those spiny trees are plush and green, and the ashes are now thick grass. The sky is powder-blue, and the air is breathable. What once was a dead place is now alive, at least on the surface. I feel the Evil beneath my feet, trapped underground. I know what it wants because all of my abilities are back. Whatever's deep down there wants to get out and reclaim what it once seized.

*Cl'auta.*

"It's Felix!" I gasp. My heart stops.

"Father?" Fawn is just as anxious as I am.

Even Zillael's eyes grow wide.

"I'm here," Felix says, rising out of the silver liquid bubbling in the gorge. He ascends wearing one of his many well-tailored, expensive black suits, unsullied by whatever that liquid is. It's easy to see that we've just gone through hell, and he hasn't.

Zillael lets go of Vayle to step beside me and loop her arm around mine. The brave warrior girl is shaking like a leaf. I reach across to rub her shoulder.

One thing about Felix—he sure knows how to make an entrance. He commands the attention of every person in the vicinity—or in this case, the forest. At first, one is mesmerized by his elegant bone structure, his straight forehead, high cheekbones, and angled chin. His eyes see right through flesh, past your spirit and into your soul. Every look he gives you is as if you're the only person he sees, and although he's slowly pulling you apart, he's reserving judgment.

As soon as he's out of the liquid, he takes deliberate steps toward us. First he examines Zillael, who tightens her grip on my arm. He comes to the perfect stop, spaced in equal measure between the five of us.

"Oh, Zillael," he says in his strong, sure way.

"Oh, Felix," she answers, intuitively knowing how to respond.

This makes him smile. "Very good." He turns his eyes on me and then Fawn. "Oh, Cl'auta, Falu."

"Oh, Felix," we reply in unison.

"This is…" He rubs his top lip as if he can't contain his joy. "A great time in history." He almost sounds choked up, which is un-Felix-like.

He stands in front of Zillael and takes her hands. Both hands are stained with blood, ashes, and other sticky stuff. She's been so busy in battle with the shadow creatures that she hasn't noticed the residue on her hands. She gasps when she finally sees it all. But Felix blows light out of his mouth and onto her hands. Once the brightness subsides, there's not a speck of anything left on them.

"There," he says, smiling at her.

Zillael gasps and lifts her hands, studying them. "Thanks. I mean, thank you."

He nods at her, his way of saying you're welcome, and turns to look at Baron. "Ze Feldis."

"Felix Parker," Baron replies.

Felix stares intensely into Baron's eyes. They may be communicating, but both of them have stellar poker faces. Never have I wished to know what a person is thinking more than I do now. Next Felix looks at Vayle, who's scowling.

"This is Jari," Felix says.

I know he's answering Vayle's thoughts. I too heard him ask, *where in the world is this place and why is he here?*

Felix studies the pool of silver liquid. "And those are the roots of the Tree of Life. If you"—he glances at Baron—"and Ze Feldis submerge yourselves in the fluid now, while it churns, you'll become what you were first created as. But"—he narrows his eyes at Vayle—"when the soil's done turning, the opportunity will pass, and you'll have to wait."

"Until when?" Vayle asks.

"The end."

Vayle still looks plenty confused. He wants to know what happens in the end and how long it will take to get there. In his mind, I see a woman with bright, inviting eyes and a sincere smile. There's a collie, and Vayle and a younger boy run across the dry autumn grass in colorful swimming trunks. They're laughing so hard they can hardly keep in a straight line. All three of them jump into what looks like a backyard lake.

"The soil will stop churning in seven hours," Felix says. "If you're human, the power of the sun has no effect."

"But I'll have my soul back?" Vayle asks.

That's when I see what he sees: darkness and a shadow that's darker than the dark. It's reaching for him, and he's paralyzed by fear. He shuts his eyes tightly as his arms, legs, and torso are pulled in different directions. The poor thing is shaking like a leaf in a tornado.

Baron and Vayle stare at each other, communicating with their eyes. They shared an experience beneath this earth.

"What are you going to do?" Vayle asks Baron.

"I'm going to do what I have to do." Although

the expression on Baron's face is assured, something is not quite right about it.

Vayle just shakes his head. "But we have a chance." It sounds as if he's trying to convince Baron to take the plunge into the turning liquid with him.

Baron nods. "I've been a vampire longer than you have. I'm the only one of our kind you know, but you're not the only one of our kind I know. There are a lot of reasons why I can't be human. The first is Clarity."

But Zillael has heard enough. She snaps her face toward Vayle. "What's your problem, guy? You have the power of the sun! There's a birthmark on your back, which means you were born with it. So do what you're supposed to do! Don't be a momma's boy!"

Felix throws up a hand. "No, Zillael, don't. Even purpose is born of free will." He casts his eyes back to Vayle. "Zillael may choose to love you, or she may not. If she chooses not, what will motivate you?"

Vayle stares into the liquid. Part of him wants to just plunge into the watery soil to get his life back and save his soul. The other part of him is considering the birthmark, what he's been able to do this far, and all that he feels for Zillael.

"I know she doesn't love me," he mutters.

"I love you," she says unconvincingly.

He scowls at her. "Don't lie to me, Zill; you love the Wek."

Zillael puckers her eyebrows. She's unable to refute that accusation. We're all hanging on the moment of silence, even Felix.

"So what now?" I ask to get us back on track.

I'm pretty sure our father showed up for a reason. He makes efficient use of his time, and showing up to congratulate us on a job well done has never been his style.

"Here are the keys to Jari," he says and flicks his wrist to toss a ball of light into the sky.

We watch the globe hang against the blue sky and then split into seven small bulbs. Three of them flutter down and penetrate the foreheads of Fawn, Zillael, and me. Three of them fly into the silver water. The last hangs over the silver pool.

"One for each daughter," Felix explains. He turns to look at the unclaimed light. "One of you is still hidden. When she's found, she'll receive the key."

He's speaking of Glo, who holds the Power of Fire.

"What do we do with the keys?" Fawn asks, taking the words right out of my mouth.

"Since Cl'auta has opened the Box of Jari, from this point on, my daughters are the only ones who can enter this universe through the main gate. It's the only entrance from Earth to Nowhere to here."

Before hundreds of exits open up all around us, leading to different parts of the world, Felix explained how Nowhere was built by the hand of Evil and will one day be destroyed by his daughters. We also learned that four years and ten months have passed on Earth since we left it. He warned us that our foes have been at work, and he assured Baron that his businesses are as secure as the day he left.

He complimented Baron on running a tight ship. "If I could have made them better, I would have, but they're already performing at their peak."

Felix pointed to two exits for Vayle: one led to Dublin, Ohio, the other to the House of Benel.

"What's in Dublin?" Vayle asked. He was crushed to hear that his mother had sold his child-hood home because it reminded her of him and moved to a new state.

We left Vayle squatting beside the churning pool and staring at the silver liquid. I didn't know what he was thinking because I decided to let his thoughts remain private. Zillael knew if she told him she loved him and pretended as though she really meant it, he'd come with us. She was the last one to leave Jari and enter the protected forest beyond our property. I turned back to watch her watch Vayle.

She couldn't bring herself to say it. After she walked through the door, it closed. That was the last we saw of Vayle.

## CHAPTER 12

# EMPTY PLACES

T t's a slow walk down the winding trails through the trees that are under the protection of the House of Benel. I think we're all lost in our heads; we haven't spoken since we left Vayle in Jari.

It's a gorgeous evening, though. Fireflies flicker against the green bushes. Birds sing to the purple sky from on their branches. The sky is clear; the moon is full and directly above us. This is the real world to me, and because I'm happy to be back in it, the image of the shadow creature, with its white eyes and canine teeth, is fading.

We pass the sculpture fountains on the lawn. As I look ahead, I see things about the house I'd never noticed. Tiny white lights are strung along the rails of the balconies, and towering poplars outline the elegant manor. The House of Benel is *home* for sure. I think my sisters feel the same way. We peel our eyes away from it to face each other. It's time to disband. Every single one of us is sweaty, grimy, and exhausted. My sisters and I are thirsty and hungry. I've never felt like this.

"So…" I mutter. I don't know what to say. I mean, what do I say after completing a journey like ours?

"I want to sleep for days." Fawn sighs.

"Me too," Zillael whispers.

Fawn half smiles at Baron. "Looks like you're the last man standing, Ze Feldis."

He tries to lift his mouth into his trademark smirk, but it comes off flat. "I guess I am."

I've already discerned that something is seriously wrong with him. He's been solemn ever since we left Jari. He hasn't taken my hand or wrapped an arm around my waist. After everything we've gone through, that's not like him.

Before I can ask if he's okay, Derek materializes in front of us as a butterfly transforms into Lorenzo. To all of our surprise, Zillael throws her arms around Derek's neck and holds him tightly. Fawn and Lorenzo stare deeply into each other's eyes.

"How about we all go get clean, rest, and pick up where we left off later?" I suggest.

We all disperse. Baron goes to the office to figure out what's happened in the time he's been gone. Zillael leans on Derek as they go off to get her cleaned, fed, and rested. I say good-bye to Fawn and Lorenzo.

When I'm back in my area, I strip out of my restrictive clothes. They're still dusty and carry evidence that Nowhere and Jari do exist. I drag into the bathroom, run a warm bath, and wash the grime of shadow creatures and patched-up corpses off of me. I wish I could read Baron's mind right now. I believe in our vow of love, and I know that whatever's wrong with him has nothing to do with me. I saw the lost souls in Vayle's mind. He's actually frightened by his own existence. I wonder if Baron feels the same way.

As I sink all the way down in the tub, I try to figure out what a good girlfriend does when her boyfriend obviously needs space to think through a traumatic experience. Do I go to his office and refuse to leave until he tells me how he's feeling? Or do I follow my own wisdom and give him space? Instead of pushing it, I finish bathing, dry off, and slip on a white tank dress with little yellow flowers.

It feels like the material baby clothes are made of, and I only wear it when I really need to feel comfortable and relaxed.

After eating a plate of berries, cream, and bread, set for me in the patio area of my space, I drag back up the stairs to the bedroom and curl up to sleep, hoping Baron feels better after I wake up.

I must have fallen asleep as soon as I closed my eyes. It's been a long time since I've dreamed of nothing at all.

When I blink my eyes into focus, I see the moon is still bright, and its wonderful rays cast soft light over me. My body doesn't ache anymore, and my limbs aren't heavy. I feel revitalized, but I'm still alone. I scoot off the bed to go look for Baron. I can feel his energy, and I know where to find him. The office he works in is all the way on the opposite side of the property. When I get to the doorway, he's deep inside the room, standing at a wide window with his back to me.

"Hey," I barely call. I feel as though I'm interrupting his privacy.

He turns around to gaze at me. "Hey." His face is lovely, and the soft look in his eyes says that he's happy to see me. "You're up."

I lean on the threshold. I love the picture of the

brooding man in a dark room. He's all cleaned up and wearing a pair of nicely fitted black trousers and a black short-sleeved tee shirt. The contrast against his fair skin is striking.

"You're in a sullen mood," I whisper and smile.

He walks over to me at regular speed. Normally he would use his vampire powers to rush across the floor in a blink of an eye. "And you're beautiful." He pulls me into him for a kiss, warm and sensual.

"Baron?"

"Yes." He consumes my bottom lip and then my top lip.

"What's wrong with you?" My eyes are closed, and I'm breathless. But I open my eyes when he stops.

He's staring at me with narrowed eyes, as though he's reading me. Is it trust he's looking for? I don't know.

"A lot," he finally confesses.

"Did something happen in Jari?"

Again, he hesitates. "Yes."

"I saw what scared Vayle. The souls. Did they frighten you as well?"

He sighs and rubs the back of his neck. Years of reading the minds of men should've stopped me from asking him if he's afraid. It's very difficult for a man to admit that to a woman he wants to protect.

"I mean, not *frighten* you," I edit. "But was there something disturbing down there?"

Baron wraps his arms around me again. "Don't worry, Clarity. I would tell you if I were afraid."

Of course he figured me out. He's naturally intuitive and has been around long enough to decipher human behavior.

"Then what is it?"

"It's not what I saw. It's who I saw. Hell, I already knew that I'm a damned bastard."

"Don't say that," I say and hold him tighter. *Gosh, he smells so good.*

"Okay, I won't say that." He kisses the top of my head. "But something's happened, Clarity."

"What's happened?"

"I was falling through the blackness. It took a while before I hit bottom. It was freezing, and I knew they were closing in. I used the light." He frowns. "They already had Vayle. They were pulling at him. He was yelling, and… it was bad."

"But they stopped when you generated the light?"

After a moment of silence, he exhales. "Yeah."

"It sounds like a sort of hell."

"It looks like it, but…"

"But what?"

"They were tugging at Vayle, but I don't think they were trying to hurt him. But he was gone, inconsolable." Again, his expression changes as he remembers those moments. "I saw Garrett, Gia, Celeste, all of them from the coven."

My heart drops to my knees. "What are you saying? They're dead?"

"I have to go see."

"Not without me."

He shakes his head. "Not this time, Clarity. It's too dangerous."

I grunt. "I'm made for danger."

"Still no."

"I'm not going to let you go alone, Baron."

"You'll still love me if I do this without your consent."

I shake my head in defiance. "Are you asking me or telling me?"

"Telling you."

I laugh a little—and cynically too. "Really? You want to play that game, Ze Feldis?" I feel myself snarling at him. "What if I just go anyway?"

"You won't do that." He sounds so sure.

"Test me."

We stare into each other's eyes. He's searching to see how determined I really am, and I'm showing him. Come hell or high water, I will go to Mount Olympus by myself if he takes off without me.

He sighs hard. "Clarity, come on." He's actually pleading with me.

"You come on." I touch his chest. It's my way of resetting us, calling a truce. "Why don't you let me go there, you know, using my"—I lift my fingers in quotes—"ability?"

"You don't know where to look. I do."

"Okay," I say. "What if I can take you with me? We've done something like that before. Remember when I first told you that Fawn could die because she fed Lario the leaf?"

Baron takes a moment to recall the occasion. "I do."

"Well, I can take your mind with me." I think about what I just said. It doesn't make sense. "Or something like that."

Baron doesn't quarrel. He's actually giving it some thought. "Let's go back to your room."

I nod. He wraps his arm around my waist as we walk at regular human speed. Again, this isn't like him.

"What else is going on with you?" I ask as our feet tap the marble floor.

"What do you mean?" he asks.

"The normalcy. You don't walk at this pace unless you have to."

His brows wrinkle.

"Tell me," I urge him.

"I don't…"

"Tell me, please?" I ask. I stop walking to face him. "Do you want me to guess?" My mouth is close to his. I don't know why the truth turns me on a little. Maybe because I feel like a woman, and there's nothing like nursing a bruised man.

"Could you guess?" he asks.

"You're not a monster, Baron." I look into his eyes.

His mouth parts; he's unable to reply. Bingo. I got it right.

"Vayle was born as a human with the mark of the sun. You were born as a human with the power of light. This *is* your destiny." I search deeper into his eyes. I think I'm reaching him. "Sometimes the path of light isn't all roses. You have to suffer. And I don't mean the sick swat-yourself-on-the-back-with-a-cat-o'-nine-tails suffer. I mean having a great

calling in life isn't all wrapped up in an uncompli-
cated package."

He's still just staring into my face, and I can't
tell what he's thinking.

I choose to take another angle in my efforts to
convince him that he's what we need him to be in
order to fight this epic battle. But before I can say
another word, his lips are on mine and his delicious
tongue tastes mine. I can feel that Baron has
decided to give in to his instincts.

In a blink of an eye, I'm lying on our bed. He's
on top of me, and his hands rub my ribs, stroke my
breasts, and move down to caress my hips. He's
watching every part of my body intensely. I'm panting. Desire makes me feel as if I'm running a
marathon.

"Clarity?"

"Yes?"

"This longing I have for you—is it man or
vampire?"

"Both," I say. "You're both."

With that, he pulls back. I watch him peel off
his shirt and then his pants. I know we're about to
make love, and I know it will mean more than it did
last time. And the next time we make love, it will

mean more than it does this time. When he's in me, we kiss.

The problem is that our mouths can't merge together. Our flesh and bones can't become one. He can't even share my soul with me. I can't share his thirst with him. I can feel his fangs throbbing against my lips. Baron Ze Feldis wants my blood. He's not thirsty, but he's a vampire. It's his nature to want it. And I'm a woman; I want to give it to him.

I'm woozy with desire, but in the back of my mind, I know we have a job to do. I feel myself peaking. Baron's thrusts are subtle, studied, as if he knows what I'm feeling and what he's doing to make that happen. At last, I cry out in ecstasy, and so does he. We hug tightly, only to stop ourselves from continuing.

"Well, that was inappropriate," I say with a chuckle.

Baron laughs softly. He knows what I'm talking about. We were in the middle of confirming the deaths of his friends before this happened.

"Where were we before you seduced me?" He jokes.

I laugh. "I don't think so."

We kiss, and my head spins.

"Okay." He takes a few breaths to calm his desire. "I had a thought."

I look into his eyes, waiting.

"Why don't I go to Greece, my way—and you follow me, your way?"

"You're changing the plans on me now?" I frown at him.

"I don't think your way will work," he says.

"But we haven't even tried it."

"Okay, but if it doesn't work, then we do it my way," he says. "I can get there in ten minutes and back."

I blink. "Ten minutes?"

"Or less," he says, sweetening the pot.

I take a moment to consider that. "Okay, deal."

Of course, Baron is right. I end up inside Celeste's room alone. As far as I can tell, the coven is vacant; I sense no signs of life.

I share this with him. His answer is to kiss me, taking the act deeper and deeper until we're making love again. After I sing with pleasure again, in a blink of an eye, Baron is gone. All I can do is wait ten minutes. Then the Encaser inside of me heads to Greece to join him.

## ZILL

"Zill, are you finishing up?" Derek calls.

I've been in the shower for close to an hour. I can't wash off the soot. Two days have gone by, and I can still smell the black ash and feel the muck and dirt on my skin. I turn off the faucet and take a deep breath before stepping out of the shower. This time I might be clean enough.

Derek has been great. He's lain with me for forty-eight hours. I've gone to sleep in his arms, woken up in his arms. He's made sure to feed me. He's petted my hair as I sobbed from time to time. I don't know why I've been crying. I think it's because things have changed, and there's no going back.

I don't want to go back to the way things were, but I'm afraid to move forward. I dry off, throw on my underwear and oversized T-shirt, and head back to bed. Two nights ago, my muscles ached something awful. But something else is strange—I'm slightly more muscular. My stomach displays a vivid six-pack. There are cuts in my shoulders and arms, even along the outsides of my thighs. I think Cl'auta was right. I was born a warrior.

However, no part of my body aches anymore. My limbs are begging me to exercise them, but my mind just wants to sleep away the memories of the icy desert, of having to go toe-to-toe, fist-to-fist with those things—*what were they?* I touched them. I killed them.

When I get to the bed, ready to crawl under the blankets, Derek rushes over to stand in front of me.

"What?" I barely ask. "I mean, what?" I say a little louder.

"How about we take a trip?"

I study those emerald eyes of his. I've known of Derek Firth since tenth grade. He's always watched me from afar, and I've always ignored him—and every other person who lived in my universe. But now I can't imagine not having those green eyes to make me feel as if I can make it through the worst that's more than likely yet to come.

"Let's go get candy apples," he suggests.

"Okay." I can't turn down what I've been craving ever since Nowhere. I think that sitting on the bench outside of Jake's Candy Apples, reliving the best day of my entire life, could be pretty therapeutic.

I heard Cl'auta the other day—well, technically five years ago—remarking on the way I dress. She's right, of course. I used to want to remain as invisible as possible. Lackluster clothing sent a message to other girls that I'm not competing and to boys that I'm not interested. That's why I fish out a pair of jeans and a pink sweater that fits. I use my sisterly wavelengths to ask Fawn for a pair of shoes. Both Clarity and that vampire of hers are way too sexy—I can't imagine wearing her clothes. Fawn is more down-to-earth. I don't like one sister more than the other, but I do know that both are *different*.

When I get to Fawn's room, she and Lorenzo are sitting on a circular sofa by a reading window. She's just finished laughing about something. Her ginger hair glistens in the sun, and her delicate, fair skin is glowing.

"You look better," she says when she looks my way.

"I think I am." I can't help but smile at her.

She walks toward me with a pair of furry tan boots. "Here."

I study them. "Thanks."

"They'll look great with what you're wearing. Try them."

Foot by foot, I put them on. *Voilà!* I look like a whole new person. Fawn agrees, and before we leave, she gives me a hug and advises me to call her and Cl'auta if I run into any fog.

Derek takes me into a tunnel and explains to me

that the ground and walls are made of diamonds. It's pretty impressive, but even this universe is too alternate for me at the moment. I need reminders of the real world. We're not in there long. We walk through an opening and enter what looks like a garage where Derek's black flatbed truck is parked. He smiles as he opens the passenger door for me. My yellow eyes connect with his green eyes.

"Thanks," I say while sliding in.

"Figured you want to travel the traditional way," he says before closing the door.

"You're right," I tell him once he slides into the driver's seat.

The last time we rode together in the truck, Derek was in a huff because he knew that I'd just lied to him about how and why I ended up at the University of Maine. I had ditched school and let Vayle lead me to the last place he'd lived as a human being.

Actually, Derek and I haven't talked about Vayle at all. A couple of days have passed since we left him at the Tree of Life. I hope we see Vayle soon no matter which form he has—man or vampire. He makes me feel just as secure as Derek.

"You want to talk about it?" Derek asks.

I take my eyes off the snow pushed up along the

side of the highway. We've already driven through a tiny town decorated with green and red tinsel, plastic candy canes, and Santa Claus heads. It's the festive time of year.

I shrug. "What is there to say?"

"You can say a lot."

I watch him. He's keeping his eyes on the road, yet his body language says he's open to listening.

"It's just… I was able to do it all so easily. It was like my mind kept feeding my body instructions. I was in control, but I had no control. Does that make sense?"

He glances at me and then stares ahead. "It's what you are, Zill, and have always been."

"Everyone keeps saying that."

"I know…"

We both look straight ahead. There are plenty of other cars on the road. It's early morning, and we're traveling north on I-95, which is strange. I'm pretty sure our house is in Vermont.

"You've been hidden until now," he says. "It was your guardian Deanna's job to keep you hidden. You were never born to live life as a human being."

"That much I can accept. It's—I tore them apart with my hands. Snatched their hearts out. Killing just comes so easy. And…"

"You don't like killing."

"No, I don't."

"You're not supposed to. That's what makes you different. You're a creature of hope, not power."

I shake my head. "I don't understand."

"Human beings seek power from the moment they're born. You were seeking hope from the moment you were conceived."

"So I kill what I'm supposed to have hope for?" I think I'm about to cry. "I feel so horrible."

"Sometimes you'll have to," he answers honestly. "But this time you didn't. The flesh mounds from the abyss were soulless, and the sand shadows, too. They were created to fight you and your sisters, and that's all."

I recognize the turn off to Moonridge. "What about you? You were doing what I was doing."

"Yes."

"So does that mean… we're in this together?"

He shoots me a glance. He's smiling. "I'm your Wek."

"And that's why we can't—you know?" My eyes are burning the side of his face.

After a moment, he says, "Yeah."

"But if you weren't my Wek, then you would— you know—with me?"

Again, he doesn't answer me right away. I don't even know why I'm asking. I already know the answer. *Dear God, I love everything about Derek.* How easy he is to talk to. How predictable he is—in a good way. He's cool, calm, and always in control. And it's not because he's a Wek. He's nothing like Lorenzo, Cl'auta's Wek. This likable being that Derek is… is just him.

"Yes, I would," he finally replies.

I'm satisfied with that answer. I don't know why, but it makes me feel more optimistic about our future. I miss Vayle, but I choose Derek. "So this is Moonridge four years later?"

We're passing the only McDonald's in town, and there are no cars in the unplowed parking lot. The lights are out, and not a soul is sitting in the booths, chomping down on the "Mac" Meals.

"Wow, did they close it down?" I wonder.

Derek studies the place just as curiously as I do. I glance at the time on the dashboard. It's 9:59 a.m.

"What's today? Do you know?"

"Thursday, December fifteenth." Derek stares straight ahead, studying those two tall mirrored-glass buildings that the mayor commissioned. What a waste of tax dollars and manpower. Boy, was he a douche.

Main Street hasn't been plowed either, and not a single car shares the road with us. No vehicles are parked at the library or at City Hall or even at a Big Lots that wasn't here four years ago. There's just a vast blanket of snow where cars and people should be.

"It's a ghost town," I mutter.

"Something's wrong." Derek pulls over to what must be the side of the road. We flow out of the truck and stand in front of it.

"Where is everybody?" I ask feebly.

Derek's eyes narrow as he looks around. "I don't know, but let's go see."

Once again, my senses are on high alert—so soon after my last hellish journey, we're finding ourselves possibly back in the thick of it.

"Maybe there's a town meeting or something?" I try to offer up a more optimistic reason why the town is deserted.

"Maybe," Derek says.

We walk past Bishop High School, and it's just as deserted as everywhere else. The ten o'clock bell buzzes. The shrieking sound of it echoes in the emptiness. *It's eerie.*

I focus on what's ahead, toward Town Square. Deep down, I'm hoping to find everyone there, engaged in one of those seasonal festivals or something. They do that here. I never attended one, but the next day at school, all the happenings of the events were all the rage. When we arrive, again we see that there are no cars parked along the road. Derek and I look at each other. I think he knows what I know.

I hear our feet crunch against the snow. We step onto the platform that lines the shops along the quad. Not a soul is present. A light wind whistles through the open air. The lights are off in Jake's Candy Apples and across the way at Molly's Apple Pies. Not one shop is open. No lights are on.

"What happened?" I can barely ask.

"Let's get out of here," Derek says.

He takes my hand before I can react, and we're up in the air. We don't even return to the truck. We're moving faster than I could go on my own, and not many seconds pass before we're back in the woods outside of our house. As we lifted off the ground, I looked back at Moonridge and saw the fog rolling in. I have no doubt we'll return, and soon. In the end, there's no rest for the weary—or candy apples.

www.ingramcontent.com/pod-product-compliance
Lightning Source LLC
Chambersburg PA
CBHW060357180626
46817CB00007B/2463